Fighting Fantasy: dare you play them all?

ASSASSINS
— OF —
ALLANSIA

IAN LIVINGSTONE

📖SCHOLASTIC

Published in the UK by Scholastic Children's Books, 2019
Euston House, 24 Eversholt Street, London, NW1 1DB, UK
A division of Scholastic Limited.

London – New York – Toronto – Sydney – Auckland
Mexico City – New Delhi – Hong Kong

ISBN 978 1407 19683 1

A CIP catalogue record for this book is available from the British Library.

Printed by CPI Group (UK) Ltd, Croydon, CR0 4YY
Papers used by Scholastic Children's Books are made
from wood grown in sustainable forests.

3 5 7 9 10 8 6 4 2

www.scholastic.co.uk

Official FIGHTING FANTASY website www.fightingfantasy.com

CONTENTS

HOW WILL YOU START
YOUR ADVENTURE?

The book you hold in your hands is a gateway to another world – a world of dark magic, terrifying monsters, brooding castles, treacherous dungeons and untold danger, where a noble few defend against the myriad schemes of the forces of evil. Welcome to the world of **FIGHTING FANTASY!**

You are about to embark upon a thrilling fantasy adventure in which **YOU** are the hero! **YOU** decide which route to take, which dangers to risk and which creatures to fight. But be warned – it will also be **YOU** who has to live or die by the consequences of your actions.

Take heed, for success is by no means certain, and you may well fail in your mission on your first attempt. But have no fear, for with experience, skill and luck, each new attempt should bring you a step closer to your ultimate goal.

Prepare yourself, for when you turn the page you will enter an exciting, perilous **FIGHTING FANTASY** adventure where every choice is yours to make, an adventure in which **YOU ARE THE HERO!**

How would you like to begin your adventure?

IF YOU ARE NEW TO FIGHTING FANTASY ...

It's a good idea to read through the rules which appear on pages 255-263 before you start.

IF YOU HAVE PLAYED FIGHTING FANTASY BEFORE ...

You'll realize that to have any chance of success, you will need to discover your hero's attributes. You can create your own character by following the instructions on pages 255–256. Don't forget to enter your character's details on the Adventure Sheet which appears on page 264.

ALTERNATIVE DICE

If you do not have a pair of dice handy, dice rolls are printed throughout the book at the bottom of the pages. Flicking rapidly through the book and stopping on a page will give you a random dice roll. If you need to 'roll' only one die, read only the first printed die; if two, total the two dice symbols.

BACKGROUND

Snake Island is a small, uninhabited island which lies between Dogfish Island and Ghost Island off the west coast of Allansia. It is rugged and inhospitable, and it is said that the reason why nobody lives there is because all those who set foot on the island are never seen again. Whether it is the terrifying creatures or undead spirits that claim the lives of visitors, nobody knows, but the rumours about Decayers, Worm Dogs and Flesh-Heads are enough to put most people off from going there. YOU have been on the island for two days, with most of the time spent making camp and foraging for food. A wager brought you to the island following a chance meeting with an old burly sea captain by the name of Samuel Crow in Port Blacksand, the notorious seaport run by the tyrant Lord Azzur. He challenged you to live on the island for a month with a wager of 20 Gold Pieces should you live to collect it. Being a brave adventurer unafraid of myths or monsters, you accepted his challenge with a shake of the hand. The captain beamed with satisfaction and slapped you on the back, saying you would regret your foolish decision. The next day, he sailed you over to Snake Island on his boat, the *Blue Moon*. It was a thrilling ride, with huge waves battering the small sailing boat as it bobbed up and down on the ocean swell. Whooping loudly as the sea spray pounded his face, the captain trimmed his sails to get as much speed as he could out of his old boat. He taunted you most of the way, saying you would survive less than twenty-four hours. But you ignored the old salt, confident that you would be more than able to deal with any danger that the island had to offer. It was mid-afternoon by the time the rocky island appeared on the horizon, and an hour later before the captain finally dropped anchor.

"Enjoy yourself," he said sarcastically, ushering you off his boat with a flick of the hand. You jumped into the cold water and waded ashore to a stony beach littered with driftwood and sun-bleached bones. You were just able to hear the captain above the noise of the waves crashing on the beach. He wished you luck with a wry grin, saying, "I'll be back in thirty days to pay you or bury you – unless you've been eaten!" You shook your fist at him with a smile and walked off to survey your new surroundings. It soon became apparent how desolate the rocky island was, evil spirits or no evil spirits. The trees were ugly, with bent trunks and gnarled, twisted branches. The thick vegetation was hostile – a tangled mix of needle-sharp thorn bushes and poisonous creepers. A cloud of mosquitoes buzzed around your head, and red ants crawled up your legs, biting you relentlessly. By the end of the day, you had encountered spiders, snakes, scorpions, ticks, grubs, leeches and other bloodsucking creatures that were going to make your life a misery in the weeks ahead. But having recently narrowly escaped with your life in Darkwood Forest, the prospect of living on an island didn't seem so bad. It would be a good place to test your survival skills, and hopefully reward you with the 20 Gold Pieces which you so desperately needed.

Leaving the stony beach behind, you walked round to the west side of the island to a small, sandy beach where you found an abandoned wooden hut nestled between some large boulders. The roof had holes in it and the door was hanging off its hinges, but with minor repairs it would be a good place to live for a month. The hut was empty apart from a dented tin jug on a small table made from driftwood, and two dirty sacks stuffed with old rags which had once been used as a makeshift bed. You fixed the door and mended the roof as best as you could as the light faded. When the sun slipped down below the horizon, the sky became a rich canvas of deep reds, vivid pinks and bright orange. The light quickly faded into total darkness, and there was nothing else to do but to lie down on the sacks and go to sleep. After spending an uncomfortable night as the target for countless mosquitoes, you wake up soon after dawn to find your whole body covered in angry red bites.

You spend the morning turning leaves and shells into rainwater traps and collecting dry wood for a fire. In the afternoon you make a chair out of driftwood fastened together with vines and a fishing rod made out of a long branch, some twine washed up on the shore, and a hook made out of a button fastening. Using limpets as bait, you manage to catch two small fish which you cook on your campfire in the dying light. Darkness falls, and day two ends the same way as day one, with you trying to get to sleep whilst being eaten alive by mosquitoes.

YOUR ADVENTURE AWAITS!

MAY YOUR STAMINA NEVER FAIL!

NOW TURN OVER...

1

The wind picks up during the night on the back of a rumbling storm which rolls in from the west. Heavy rain turns into a torrential downpour and beats down noisily on the roof. Rainwater finds its way through your roof repairs and drips down on to the floorboards. You hear strange noises coming from outside, with the howling wind playing tricks on your imagination in the pitch-black darkness. The storm eventually passes, and you finally drift off to sleep, but in the middle of the night you suddenly wake up with a start. The wind has dropped, and you can hear the sound of waves breaking on the beach. But you hear another sound much closer – a tiny squeak – and one which you recognize. Somebody is trying to open the door. Who could it be? Nobody else lives on this forsaken island. It's too dark to see anything. You stand up slowly, sword in hand and heart pounding, hardly daring to breathe. If you want to stand still where you are, turn to **356**. If you want to go outside to investigate, turn to **161**.

2

The warrior's aim is deadly accurate, but you just manage to raise your shield in time to meet the spear, which clatters off and falls harmlessly to the ground. The warrior is only twenty metres away and closing in fast, wielding two long knives. If you want to reach for her spear and throw it back at her, turn to **96**. If you want to draw your sword and ready yourself for combat, turn to **266**.

3

The Monk berates you for wasting his time. If you want to attack him with your sword, turn to **260**. If you would rather ignore him and walk across the market square to Clock Street, turn to **140**.

4

You raise your sword and strike the Orc a mighty blow in its midriff as it runs past the tree you are hiding behind. It stops in its tracks and falls to the ground with blood pouring from its stomach. It is badly injured but manages to get back up on its feet. Roaring in pain, it staggers towards you, spitting blood and swinging its morning star. You must finish off the Orc quickly before the other Orcs hear the commotion.

ORC   *SKILL 6*   *STAMINA 2*

If you win the fight in the first Attack Round, turn to **311**. If it takes two or more Attack Rounds to defeat the Orc, turn to **193**.

5

From where you are lying, you have a good view of the ship's mast and the lone lookout standing in the crow's nest. The lookout suddenly becomes agitated and calls down to the crew on deck, yelling at them to look west. You hear the pirate captain order his helmsman to turn his ship hard right, which makes the *Blue Moon* take on water as it rolls from side to side and causes you to bang your head. Lose 1 *STAMINA* point. You decide the best thing to do to avoid being sunk is to cut the tow rope. Turn to **88**.

Two Dwarfs wearing horned helmets

You reach for the idol and hear a click. An unseen trapdoor suddenly gives way under your feet and you fall through it, landing on the cellar floor and banging your head. Lose 2 *STAMINA* points. Lying on the damp floor in pain, you are plunged into darkness when the trapdoor is pulled back up and bolted. It seems like an age before the trapdoor opens again, whereupon you see two DWARFS wearing horned helmets staring down at you with curious expressions on their faces. They are identical twins with long ginger hair tied in plaits, beards, moustaches, eyes set close together, missing front teeth and big, hairy noses which they are both picking furiously. One of them stops picking his nose for a moment and says in a long, drawn-out voice, "Well, brother Billy, who have we caught trespassing?"

"No idea, brother Bobby."

"Is it somebody we know?"

"Nobody I know. Is it somebody you know?"

"No."

"Well, somebody must know!"

"You could always ask."

"I will," says Billy. "Hey, you down there, who do you think you are coming into our house without being asked? Did you not read the sign outside? Let me tell you that we are the Bogg brothers. I'm Billy Bogg and this here is my brother Bobby Bogg. We don't like visitors, and we really hate trespassers. What have you got to say for yourself?"

If you want to reply that you were looking to buy some food, turn to **38**. If you want to tell them that you are on the run from assassins, turn to **291**.

7

You take aim and hurl the meat cleaver at the pirate as hard as you can. It is a miracle shot and strikes the pirate on the side of the head, knocking him out. He slumps forward on to the deck and lets go of the sailing ropes. The *Blue Moon* drifts to a halt, and you are able to catch up with it and climb on board. The scraggy-looking pirate slowly comes around, moaning and groaning. You tie his hands behind his back and ask him why you shouldn't throw him in the sea to feed to the Blood Sharks. "I know who you are. I saw your face on a poster in Port Blacksand," the pirate says gruffly. "I've got something you need. Let me live and I will tell you what it is." You tell him to keep talking and you'll think about it. "I know the assassins are hunting you, and there's one who will try to poison you with snake venom. See my earring? It's a Snakefang. Wear it, and you won't come to any harm from snake venom." If you want to take the pirate's earring and wear it, turn to **37**. If you do not want to take the earring, turn to **296**.

8

You come to the foot of a hill and begin to breathe heavily as you run up it. The chasing Orcs charge up the hill without breaking step and are now only metres behind you. Exhausted, you turn to face them. Turn to **230**.

9

Back on dry land, you slip your hand inside the leather straps on the back of the shield. You feel a sudden surge of power run up your arm. You have found the Shield of the Sentinels. Add 1 *SKILL* point and 1 *LUCK* point. Pleased with your new piece of armour, you gather up your belongings and climb back up the stone steps to the top of the cliff. Turn to **127**.

10

Billy smiles and says, "That seems like a fair offer to me, brother Bobby. Throw the rope down to our new friend." You pick up the assassin's axes and climb out of the cellar and are greeted by the brothers, who slap you on the back. "No hard feelings, I hope?" says Billy. You shake your head and hand him an axe, a ring and 9 Gold Pieces. The brothers shake your hand and walk with you to the wooden gate, where they bid you farewell. You wave goodbye and set off again towards Kaad. Turn to **307**.

11

You fill the tin jug with water from the rainwater traps outside and can't stop thinking about the attempt on your life. After quenching your thirst, you decide to go in search of food. You are very hungry, having eaten only a bit of fish the previous day. Lose 1 *STAMINA* point. If you want to go fishing again, turn to **34**. If you want to explore the island for food, turn to **116**.

12

You undo the clasp and open the book to find that all the pages are hollowed out of the middle and there is a finely engraved gold ring wrapped in wool lying in the cavity. There are no words in the book other than an instruction on the title page penned in elaborate italic gold writing, which reads, *Kiss the Warp Ring to go back one minute in time. Choose your moment carefully because this can be done but once.* The chance to go back in time is impossible to resist and you slip the ring on to your middle finger. You turn it round and round on your finger as you walk back up the stairs to go outside with your mind spinning, thinking about what it might be like to go back in time. Turn to **305**.

13

You raise your arm just in time as the piercing arrow clatters into your shield and ricochets away. Your assailant reloads and fires again, but you manage to deflect the second arrow. With your sword drawn, you charge at your attacker, who throws back her hood to reveal the unmistakable features of a DARK ELF PRIESTESS. Her neck is covered with tattoos of writhing serpents and her long ice-white hair is tied up high on her head. She is wearing studded leather armour with iron-plated shoulder pads. Staring at you with cold, amethyst-blue eyes, she draws her long sword slowly from its scabbard, a shimmering blade made of the finest Salamonian steel enveloped in a swirling mist of vivid colours. Swinging it skilfully above her head, the Dark Elf advances towards you, meeting your sword with a clash of steel, her chilling war cry sending a shiver down your spine.

DARK ELF PRIESTESS   *SKILL 8*   *STAMINA 8*

If you win, turn to **61**.

14

You climb into the back of the open carriage, and the driver cracks his whip in the air to spur his horse into a trot. The woman turns to you as you speed along the dusty track and says, "My name is Florence Figgins. I'm the town's undertaker. I am on my way to Anvil to visit relatives. The chances are we won't get there before nightfall, but Henry here is more than capable of defending me from the creatures of the Pagan Plain. Now sit back and enjoy the ride. We should be at Otto's within the hour." The light begins to fade and by the time the carriage comes to a halt outside a log cabin, shadows are already creeping over the land. "Welcome to Otto's Outpost," Florence says warmly. "This is as far as you go with us. I hope you manage to track down Lord Azzur before he returns to Port Blacksand. Good luck." You jump down from the carriage and thank Florence for the ride. She snaps her fingers and her driver cracks his whip to send the horse into a gallop, and you watch the carriage disappear in a cloud of dust towards the setting sun. The log cabin looks to be well built and secured with wooden shutters on all the windows. There is a wooden sign above the door which reads OTTO'S OUTPOST. It's been a grisly day and you are relieved to find shelter. Turn to **264**.

15

Apart from the boat being rocked by a school of Blubber Whales swimming close by, the voyage passes without incident. You sail along the rugged Allansian coastline until you come to an estuary which you know to be the entrance to Red River. You sail a short distance up the river to where there are two wooden buildings on the northern bank. You steer the *Blue Moon* over to the bank, jump out, and tie it up to a small dock. It feels good to be back on dry land, but you are also very aware that Lord Azzur will not rest until one of his assassins has delivered your head to him. If only Captain Crow had told you who the other assassins were before he died, you would be better prepared. Now you suspect everybody you meet could be an assassin. But at least you should recognize Garanka Vassell when you see him. You walk towards the buildings, which you note are a boatyard and a general store. Thinking you might be able to sell the *Blue Moon*, you decide to visit the boatyard first. Turn to **288**.

16

You come to a small sunlit glade where lots of exotic wild flowers are blooming. You walk through the glade but become anxious when you suddenly feel the ground tremble. You are thrown off your feet by a violent tremor and carried up into the air on a bed of soil engulfed in the jaws of a GIANT SLUGWORM which rises out of the ground. Its massive tubular body rises five metres into the air before it closes its jaws to swallow you whole. Everything goes dark. Your adventure is over.

17

A thick glob of drool flies past your head, just missing you. You do not stop to look back and you run through the undergrowth as fast as you can. Turn to **213**.

18

You run as fast as you can, but you are breathing hard after the gruelling battle with the Orc. You look round to see the chasing band of Orcs is slowly closing in on you. If you are carrying a Bag of Everything, turn to **94**. If you are carrying an ordinary backpack, turn to **376**.

19

The old man, who you notice has a bald pate and a ring on every finger, stops in his tracks and begins speaking cheerfully in rhyming couplets.

"No doubt the reason you've stopped me here
Is because it can't be me you fear
Perhaps you think my sack contains
Treasure, gold or illicit gains?
Banish all thoughts of theft and plunder
That would be an enormous blunder
I might look old and frail and tragic
But I'm a Monk with the power of deadly magic."

The old man folds his arms across his chest and starts

tapping his right foot impatiently, waiting for you to speak. If you want to ask him if there is anything in his sack that he would like to sell, turn to **211**. If you want to attack him with your sword, turn to **260**.

20

The blacksmith puts down his ladle and picks up his stone hammer. "Horseshoes? Don't take me for a fool. Where's your horse? Get out of here before I kick you out!" Rather than argue with the angry blacksmith, you go back outside and walk down the side passage. Turn to **330**.

21

The pirate ship is fast closing in on the *Blue Moon*, and you let go of the ropes to let the sail flap as though the boat is adrift. The pirates will be eager to find out if you have anything worth stealing, and your pretending to be dead might not deter them from finding out. If you possess a bottle of red ink, turn to **180**. If you do not have any ink, turn to **95**.

22

You are relieved to have survived another assassination attempt. The first thing that catches your eye is the warrior woman's silver necklace with the now familiar scorpion pendant hanging from her neck. You snatch it from her

The storekeeper looks over the top of his wire-rimmed spectacles

and place it in your pocket with the others. You also take the snake-shaped gold armband from her right bicep and empty her leather pouch, which contains 2 Gold Pieces. If you want to try on the armband, turn to **318**. If you would rather place it in your backpack, turn to **139**.

23

A bell rings when you open the door, and you see a curly-haired man behind a counter putting canvas backpacks on a shelf. All the shelves are crammed with hats, gloves, boots, belts, water flasks, rope and general camping equipment. The floor is covered with sacks, barrels and boxes filled with bread, vegetables, grain and dried foodstuffs. A glass display case on the counter contains some interesting-looking objects with runes and mysterious symbols on them. The storekeeper looks over the top of his wire-rimmed spectacles, smiles and says, "Well, well, well, if it isn't Lord Azzur's favourite person! I recognize your face. What brings you here?" Will you:

Reply that you don't know what he's talking about?	Turn to **58**
Say that you want to buy some Provisions?	Turn to **64**
Ask him if he sells Elven Boots?	Turn to **317**
Smile politely and leave the store to head east on foot?	Turn to **203**

24

You give a quick wave to the angry crew, turn, and dive over the back of the ship. You soon reach the *Blue Moon*, which is under tow in the wake of the pirate ship. You grab hold of the side and haul yourself on board. You know your only chance of survival is to act quickly and cut the rope attached to the grappling hook. Turn to **88**.

25

Azzur looks at you with contempt and says in a sinister voice, "Miserable worm. You failed to kill them all. Look behind you!" Before you have time to turn, your head is cleaved from your neck by a flashing blade. A huge cheer erupts from the excited crowd, many of whom have travelled far to see blood spilled today. Lord Azzur puts his arm around his assassin and says, "Congratulations. Not only have you earned my reward of 1,000 Gold Pieces, but you have also earned the right to represent me in Deathtrap Dungeon today. You will earn another 1,000 Gold Pieces of the prize money – if you survive!" The assassin bows to Lord Azzur and Baron Sukumvit raises his arm for the trumpets to signal the start of this year's Trial of Champions. The crowd goes wild, and one by one the contestants salute the Baron and run through the ornate stone-pillared dungeon entrance and disappear into the darkness. Your adventure is over.

26

You hand over 2 Gold Pieces to Tall Tom, which brings a big smile to his face. "Thank you," he says happily. "I should also thank you for getting rid of Vassell. He was an all-round disgusting human being. He was rude, ate like a pig and his room stank. I could hardly believe it when he told me he was an assassin working for Lord Azzur! He showed me a 'Wanted' poster and told me he was going to chop your head off! He said that you might be coming here and that there were other assassins looking for you, although he was convinced he would win the 1,000 Gold Piece bounty. So much for that plan! But the others will undoubtedly pick up your trail. Now you don't look like a murderer to me, and the only way you can stop this is to find Lord Azzur and convince him to call off his dogs. So, what I suggest is, why don't you speak to Sidd the Seer over there? He's a little strange, but he sees things nobody else sees." You look over at the eccentric-looking man sitting at the table who smiles nervously and then looks away again. Will you:

Go over to talk to Sidd?	Turn to **74**
Leave the tavern and head north?	Turn to **133**
Leave the tavern and continue east?	Turn to **157**

27

You lose your footing and fall off the path, tumbling head over heels on to the beach below. You land on a patch of soft sand but are winded and twist your ankle badly. Lose 1 *SKILL* point and 2 *STAMINA* points. You look up to see the Flesh-Head peering down over the cliff edge, snarling aggressively. You stand up, winded and in considerable pain, and walk gingerly over to the mouth of the cave. Turn to **201**.

28

The door isn't locked and opens into a large room which smells of sewage and looks like it hasn't been cleaned in years. Old bones, dirty clothes, broken furniture, cracked plates, mouldy cheese, rotten meat, empty bottles and two dead dogs are piled up on both sides of a narrow walkway to the back of the room, where there is a filthy iron stove encrusted with burnt food. A blackened pot of cabbage water is bubbling away on the stove and there is, strangely, a golden idol in the shape of a pig on the shelf above it. If you want to take the idol, turn to **6**. If you would rather walk back to the entrance gate and head towards Kaad, turn to **307**.

29

The boat man glares at you and says, "I told you my offer was 20 Gold Pieces. That was a fair price. Now it's 15 Gold Pieces." You try to argue with him, but he threatens to drop his offer to 10 Gold Pieces. You reluctantly accept the offer of 15 Gold Pieces, which he counts out into your hand coin by coin. With the transaction done, he turns and walks back into his yard with his dogs following faithfully behind. If you now want to go in the general store, turn to **327**. If you would rather head east on foot immediately, turn to **203**.

30

The man shrugs and says, "Oh, that's a pity, but never mind. So, what can I do for you?" If you want to say that you have come to return a box that you believe belongs to him, turn to **386**. If you want to ask if he has seen Lord Azzur in town, turn to **167**.

31

The man smiles and pulls out a mini crossbow from inside his coat and fires it at you. *Test Your Luck*. If you are Lucky, turn to **374**. If you are Unlucky, turn to **175**.

32

If you want to sell your old pair of leather boots, turn to **384**. If you have a pair of Elven Boots and want to sell them, turn to **324**.

33

Relieved to have survived another assassination attempt, you reach down to open Red Ruth's cloak and find a silver necklace around her neck with a scorpion pendant hanging from it. You break the chain and place the pendant in your pocket with the others. How many more assassins are out there, you ask yourself. You can only speculate as you walk up the passageway which leads on to Brick Street. If you want to go left and walk to the next junction, turn to **137**. If you would rather turn right and walk towards a small group of people who are standing at a crossroads, turn to **396**.

34

You spend two hours casting your line into the sea but fail to catch a single fish. The sea is rough, and the fish aren't biting. Lose 1 *STAMINA* point and 1 *LUCK* point. If you want to carry on fishing, turn to **382**. If you would rather explore the island, turn to **116**.

35

The woman curses and says, sneering, "You are right to be suspicious of me, stranger. I am not Frances Fletcher. The real arrow maker had an unfortunate accident recently and is sadly no longer with us. My name is Gretta Morg. I am an assassin sent by Lord Azzur. Prepare to die!" The assassin reaches behind her and pulls out two short swords from sheaths hidden behind her back. You must fight her to the death.

GRETTA MORG   *SKILL 8*   *STAMINA 7*

If you win, turn to **321**.

36

Your hands are shackled behind your back, and you are made to stand bleeding and battered in front of the baying crowd to await your fate. Baron Sukumvit orders his Guards to remove your helmet, and the crowd gasps when your face is revealed. Lord Azzur stares at you coldly, unmoved by the attack. The Baron turns to his guest and says, "My sincere apologies for this outrage, my dear Lord Azzur. As punishment, might I suggest we put this criminal in the iron gibbet hanging from the gallows in the town square and let the hungry crows do the rest?" Lord Azzur gives his approval with a simple gesture of the hand. You are dragged from the podium but manage to catch Throm's eye and mouth "good luck" to him. Whilst his fate is unknown, for you, the gallows await. Your adventure is over.

37

You take the earring and see that it has been made out of snake fangs. You fix it to your ear, wary that it might be a trick, but nothing untoward happens. "You'll thank me for this one day," the pirate says with a sneer. He asks you to untie him, but you refuse, saying that you will set him free only when you approach landfall. You trim the sail and set a course away from the sea monster, which could appear again at any moment. If you want to head due east towards the Red River estuary, turn to **345**. If you would rather sail south-east to Port Blacksand, turn to **393**.

38

Brother Bobby rubs his chin and says, "Why would you say that? Any fool can see our crops are rotten! What do you think, brother Billy?" Billy rubs his chin and says, "You make a good point, brother Bobby. What I want to know is why was this sneak thief standing by the oven? Was it that maybe they had their eye on our little piggy? What say you down there?" If you want to insist that you were hoping to buy some food, turn to **240**. If you want to admit that you were going to steal the golden idol, turn to **143**.

"My name is Zeedle. I am the Ferryman of Fang."

39

You tap the brass bell with the edge of your sword. It rings out sharply and the man sits up with a start. He has long hair sticking out from under his woollen hat, and a lined and weathered face. His black woolen jumper matches his hat, and he smiles warmly as he steps on to the jetty, saying, "Good morning. My name is Zeedle. I am the Ferryman of Fang. For 1 Gold Piece I will gladly row you across the river. Please step aboard. I would advise against swimming across since this part of the river is teeming with flesh-eating Snapperfish." Will you:

Pay Zeedle 1 Gold Piece?	Turn to **77**
Punch him in the face?	Turn to **132**
Swim across the river?	Turn to **155**

40

The bracelet used to belong to an infamous pirate called "Stumpy" Stanley Stubbs who died at sea from food poisoning. His loot was shared out by his crew, including the bracelet, which was taken by a deckhand by the name of Jack Jamlo who later came to Snake Island and was never seen again. What neither of them knew is that the bracelet had been cursed by a blind Witch so that bad luck would come to all those who wore it, including you. Lose 5 *LUCK* points. Unaware of the curse, you are pleased with the bracelet, and head west back to your hut on the other side of the island. Turn to **217**.

41

The chicks stop screeching and you look down and see the Orc walk past the tree. You breathe a sigh of relief and climb down the tree when he is out of sight. You make your way quickly north to get as far away as you can from the Orcs. But just when you think you have escaped, a long blast on a hunting horn signals that you have been spotted by one of their scouts. You hear a loud roar behind you and the thunder of heavy footsteps of the band of Orcs giving chase. All you can do is run. If you are wearing Elven Boots, turn to **241**. If you are wearing ordinary leather boots, turn to **18**.

42

The assassin sees you running towards the tavern. He aims his crossbow at you and fires. The bolt thumps into your thigh with a dull thud. Lose 2 *STAMINA* points. The pain is terrible, and unable to run, you stop to pull the bolt out. But there is no time to treat the wound, as the tavern door suddenly bursts open. A heavily built man wearing a chain mail vest storms out of the tavern, screaming at the top of his voice, and charges at you like a raging bull, swinging a two-handed sword above his head. You draw your sword and ready yourself to fight the deadly assassin, Garanka Vassell. Turn to **53**.

43

You draw your sword and launch yourself at the giant carnivorous plant, hacking furiously at its proboscis. The fibrous texture is tough to cut through, and poor Captain Crow howls in agony each time you strike it. You finally manage to cleave through it, causing the vines to loosen their iron-like grip on the captain. You extract the proboscis from the captain's throat, but there is nothing you can do to save him. Whilst burying the captain, you see the proboscis of another Bloodwort creeping towards you, which you skewer with your sword. You walk back to the beach deep in thought and inadvertently step on a nest of Giant Fire Ants. Hundreds of ants swarm up your legs and sting you multiple times, injecting you with poisonous venom. Lose 2 *STAMINA* points. You run back to the beach as fast as you can, picking up a piece of wood on the way to replace the broken tiller. Still covered in ants, you wade straight out to sea to wash them off before jumping on board the *Blue Moon*. It doesn't take long to repair the broken tiller and, job done, you let out the mainsail and cast off. Turn to **71**.

44

Much to your relief, the key turns in the lock. You release the iron catch holding the trap shut and free your ankle. After bandaging the wound, you continue on your way and eventually come to a rickety old gate on the right which has a large sign nailed to it with the words BOGG FARM – BOG OFF painted on it. A gravel path leads from the gate to an old farmhouse, which sits in the middle of a small field separated from the grassland by a wooden fence. There is a stone post next to the gate with an arrow carved on it pointing towards the town and the words KAAD – 1 MILE underneath. From this distance, Kaad looks like it is a small town. The buildings are few in number and are mostly one or two storeys high except a stone tower in the centre of town. If you want to open the gate and walk up the path to the farmhouse, turn to **70**. If you would rather continue on to Kaad, turn to **307**.

45

The path alongside the river takes you through a wooded area beyond which there is a wooden building in the distance. As you get close, you see a sign above the front door which says TALL TOM'S TAVERN. If you talked to Harold Cornpepper about Tall Tom's Tavern, turn to **197**. If you didn't talk to him about the tavern, turn to **166**.

46

You aren't strong enough to pull the skeleton hand away, and the bony fingers sink deeper and deeper into your throat. Lose 1 *SKILL* point and 2 *STAMINA* points. Gasping for air, you are on the verge of passing out and summon all your remaining strength to pull the hand away from your throat. Roll two dice. If the number rolled is less than or equal to your *SKILL* score, turn to **214**. If the number rolled is greater than your *SKILL* score, turn to **337**.

47

The path veers away from the tributary and goes into a wooded area. You make your way carefully through the wood, ever alert for assassins who might be lying in wait to ambush you. You follow the path up a gentle hill and down the other side to where the wood opens out on to a large grass-covered plain. You see that the path continues north towards a forest and is met by another path heading north-east towards a town in the far distance. If you want to stay on the path heading north towards the forest, turn to **101**. If you want to walk to the junction and take the new path heading towards the town, turn to **200**.

48

You walk up to the men and see them pull long knives from inside their clothing. On the wall behind them, you see a "Wanted" poster with your face on it. The THIEVES know who you are, and you have no option but to fight them.

	SKILL	STAMINA
First THIEF	7	7
Second THIEF	6	8

Fight them one at a time. If you win, turn to **184**.

49

Silence descends over the crowd. Azzur plays to the audience, rubbing his chin as though appearing to be deep in thought. "That's a good number," he says coldly. "But it's not good enough!" Turn to **25**.

50

The Worm Dog's saliva is infected with a deadly virus. If you possess a bottle of Worm Paste, turn to **192**. If you do not have any Worm Paste, turn to **227**.

51

The little man shakes his head in disbelief and watches you disappear into the forest. You hear him call out,

"You'll be sorry," but ignore his warning. The thick foliage overhead cuts out much of the sunlight and makes the forest very dark and gloomy. It's hard work finding a way through the trees and dense undergrowth, and you keep stumbling over roots that are hidden by a thick covering of leaves. If you wish to press on regardless, turn to **16**. If you would rather retrace your steps and head east along the edge of the forest towards Kaad, turn to **328**.

52

You hear the click of the trigger, but the pistol misfires with the flint failing to ignite the powder in the chamber. The captain curses and draws his cutlass, telling his crew to stand back. "Leave this scurvy rat to me," he says in a gruff voice.

PIRATE CAPTAIN   *SKILL 8*   *STAMINA 8*

If you win, turn to **239**.

His longsword is held high above his head

53

Garanka Vassell is in a violent rage with his mad eyes bulging in their sockets and his tongue sticking out of his gold-toothed mouth. He runs at you, screaming loudly, his chain mail vest glistening in the sun. His longsword is held high above his head, gripped firmly in his enormous hands, and he brings it down to strike you with all his brutish might.

GARANKA VASSELL   *SKILL 10*   *STAMINA 9*

If you win, turn to **387**.

54

There are four items in the display case which especially catch your eye. A gold bracelet etched with a sun symbol, a runic scroll, a silver ring with a ruby centre stone and a brass flute. "I see you've got your eye on a couple of things," the storekeeper says, eagerly rubbing his hands together. "Let me tell you about them. The Bracelet of Power will increase your fighting ability (add 3 *SKILL* points). The Scroll of Invisibility will enable you to turn invisible for a minute. Just hold the scroll out in front of you and utter the words 'Now you see me, now you don't.' The Ring of Healing will restore your health (add 6 *STAMINA* points). The Magic Flute always plays the same song no matter what notes you play, but I don't know what it is. Each item costs 5 Gold Pieces or you can have all four for 15 Gold Pieces. Interested?" If you want to buy one or more of the items, pay the storekeeper the amount and make a note of your purchases. You thank him for his help and leave the store to head east in pursuit of Garanka Vassell. Turn to **203**.

55

You run up the street with the townsfolk chasing after you, shouting and waving their fists. If you want to run down an alleyway up ahead on the right, turn to **150**. If you have two Gold Pieces and want to throw them in the air to distract the chasing pack, turn to **113**.

56

You hear a faint click when you lift up the lid. You flinch, half expecting a poison dart to shoot out, but nothing happens. Inside the chest you find a leather purse tied shut, and a small silver box. Will you:

Open the leather purse?	Turn to **319**
Open the silver box?	Turn to **377**
Close the chest and scour the beach?	Turn to **231**

57

The heat subsides, and you immediately feel sharper and more powerful. You are wearing a Mamba Band with its snake-like magic powers which will increase your energy and improve your reflexes. Add 2 *SKILL* points, 2 *STAMINA* points and 1 *LUCK* point. Pleased with your find, you think about which way to head. If you want to keep going north, turn to **87**. If you want to head east along the new path, turn to **222**.

58

The storekeeper looks at you and says dismissively, "Don't give me that nonsense. Who are you trying to fool? Your face is on the poster outside. Don't lie to me or I'll be tempted to have a go at claiming the 1,000 Gold Pieces myself! You need my help, but now it's going to cost you 1 Gold Piece to stop me from closing my store and going home." If you want to pay the storekeeper, turn to **91**. If you would rather tell him to whistle for his Gold Piece and leave the store to head east on foot, turn to **203**.

59

The Assassin's dagger is coated with deadly frog poison, and although you only suffer a slight flesh wound, you drop to the ground feeling as though your blood is boiling. You begin to shake uncontrollably and soon pass out, never to regain consciousness. Your adventure is over.

60

When she sees you draw your sword, the assassin curses and pulls out two short swords from sheaths hidden behind her back. You must fight her to the death.

GRETTA MORG   *SKILL 8*   *STAMINA 7*

If you win, turn to **321**.

61

With blood trickling from her mouth, the Dark Elf still manages a contemptuous smile, and says in her dying breath, "I might have failed . . . but one of our guild will see you dead." With that, her head slumps to one side, and she falls silent. You notice that she is wearing the same silver necklace and scorpion pendant as the bearded man who tried to kill you the previous night. You snatch it from her neck and put it in your pocket. "Bravo!" you hear a voice call out cheerfully. You turn and walk over to the *Blue Moon*, where you find Captain Crow chained to the mast. "That was impressive. I never thought you would get the better of Oleander Redfly. Now, if you don't mind, would you please release me from these wretched chains? The key is in there," he says, pointing at a wooden box on the foredeck. After freeing the captain, you ask him why people are trying to kill you. You show him the pendants and tell him about last night's attempt on your life. "That would have been Tarrak Kazan. He's an assassin," he says matter-of-factly. "Kazan won the right to have the first chance to assassinate you." The captain sees the puzzled expression on your face and begins a detailed account of what happened to him since he left you to fend for yourself on Snake Island. He recounts how he sailed back to Port Blacksand, where he saw "Wanted" posters plastered all over the city with a drawing of your face on them and a bounty of 1,000 Gold Pieces being offered by Lord Azzur for your head. The captain foolishly told the innkeeper at the Rusty Anchor Inn, where he was staying, that you had been sailing with him earlier that day. The innkeeper grunted as though uninterested, but the next morning the captain was hauled away by Imperial Guards to Lord Azzur's palace to face his cruel interrogators. "Threatened with torture," he says, "I had no option but to tell the pig-faced brutes that I knew where you were. As soon as Lord Azzur found out, he stormed into the room and started screaming at me and kicking me for helping a prime suspect leave Port Blacksand. Whether or not it was true, his spies had told him that you had killed his master, Zanbar Bone. Now, I'm no fan of Zanbar Bone, and I say good riddance to the Demon Prince, but what was I supposed to do? I had no choice but to tell him that I had taken you to Snake Island. When he finished kicking me, Azzur sent for his best assassins from the notorious Scorpion Guild of Assassins to hunt you down. Kazan and Redfly might be dead, but there will be more assassins coming after you, I'm afraid. I watched them coolly draw straws to decide who would go first to hunt you down. Tarrak Kazan drew the longest straw and set off immediately. As we know, he didn't return with your head! The next day I was forced to sail back to Snake Island with Oleander Redfly on board, the next assassin in line to kill you. She boasted that she had assassinated many hapless victims and you would be next, but clearly she was wrong!" the captain says with gusto. "The problem we now have is that since Redfly will not return to the palace with your head this evening, Azzur will send out his next assassin to claim the bounty. He might be impatient enough to send them all out at once to hunt you down! On our voyage here, Redfly said that she was lucky to go second, as the assassins following her were the meanest, cruellest and most brutal assassins in all Allansia. I really feared for your life when she told me about a couple of them, particularly an ex-mercenary fighter called Garanka Vassell. His speciality is removing a victim's head from their shoulders with one swipe of his two-handed sword. I've never seen a more mean-looking brute. He had a dent in his skull caused by a war-hammer blow, and he also had a mouthful of gold teeth. We should leave Snake Island soon before Vassell pays us a visit! But I don't think right now is the time to be going to sea. Look, there's a storm brewing," the captain says, pointing at the darkening sky. "What do you want to do?" If you want to spend another night on the island, turn to **302**. If you want to tell Captain Crow to set sail immediately, turn to **182**.

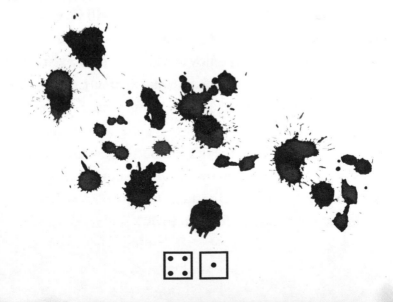

62

A crossbow bolt flies past your head and slams into a tree trunk with a dull thud. You spin round and see the tavern door burst open. A bald-headed man wearing a chain mail vest storms out of the tavern screaming, and charges at you like a raging bull, swinging a two-handed sword above his head. You notice that he has a dent in his skull and all his teeth are made of gold. It is the deadly assassin Garanka Vassell and you must fight him. Turn to **53**.

63

You follow the woman down a flight of narrow steps to a candlelit tunnel which ends at a wooden door. The woman turns to you and says, "My inner eye told me you were in danger. You'll be safe here. Your face is familiar, but I can't place it. Have we met before? Perhaps it will come to me later. But no matter. You should be able to leave soon but, in the meantime, please enjoy my secret hideaway. It is my special place of solitude where I come to practise my magic powers. There is so much energy underground! Come, let me show you my books of magic." The woman walks to the end of the tunnel, pushes open the wooden door and disappears through the doorway. If you want to follow her, turn to **224**. If you would rather walk quickly back up the steps and go back outside, turn to **305**.

64

The storekeeper listens to you sympathetically as you relate the events of the past few days and says, "That is terrible. You look like you haven't eaten in ages! I make the best bread in the land, and I stock the tastiest cheese and tomatoes in Allansia. I'll sell you a fresh loaf, a big chunk of cheese and some ripe tomatoes for just 1 Gold Piece. If you need something special to put the food in, I'll also sell you a wizard's backpack for a bargain price of 4 Gold Pieces. It's a Bag of Everything. No matter what you put in it, it will always feel as light as a feather." Will you:

Buy the food for 1 Gold Piece?	Turn to **105**
Buy the food and the backpack for 5 Gold Pieces?	Turn to **364**
Decline his offer?	Turn to **215**

65

You jump on to the podium and are immediately set upon by the Baron's elite Guards, who rain blow after blow down on you with their iron maces, clubbing you to the ground.

If you are wearing a Warp Ring, turn to **130**. If you are not wearing this ring, turn to **36**.

66

You land heavily on the sand and sprain your shoulder. You also suffer a twisted ankle and two cracked ribs. Lose 3 *SKILL* points and 6 *STAMINA* points. If you are still alive, turn to **392**.

67

Bobby tells you to throw your sword up to him together with the Gold Pieces. "You can collect the carving and your sword by the entrance gate where brother Billy will leave them. I'm going to throw a rope down for you to climb up, so you can be on your way. No funny business, mind, or you'll feel the sharp end of my blunderbuss!" Minutes later a thick rope drops down into the cellar. Satisfied it will bear your weight, you climb out of the cellar, but the brothers are nowhere to be seen. You waste no time and walk back to the wooden gate, where you see your sword and the gold-painted pig. You look back at the farmhouse and see the brothers sitting on the roof with Bobby holding his blunderbuss. They give you the thumbs up and begin laughing so hard they almost fall off the roof. You decide it best to leave them to it and bandage your leg before heading for Kaad. Turn to **307**.

68

You tap the man on the shoulder, and when he sits up, his hat falls off and you see he is not a human but an ugly GOBLIN with a huge nose and green warty skin. A weighted net suddenly falls down on top of you, dropped from above by a second Goblin standing on a high branch. The first Goblin springs to his feet, giggling with glee as you struggle to free yourself from underneath the heavy rope net. Roll two dice. If the total is equal to or less than your *SKILL* score, turn to **308**. If the number is greater than your *SKILL* score, turn to **342**.

The ugly brutes have green warty skin

69

The noise of marching feet and singing grows steadily louder, and it's not long before you see a band of leather-armoured creatures march into the clearing. The ugly brutes have green warty skin and blackened tusks protruding from their large mouths. Your nostrils twitch when the foul smell of their unwashed bodies wafts over on the breeze. You recognize the smell from previous encounters, as there is nothing more unpleasant than the putrid smell of an ORC's armpit combined with the hideous stench of the gas they release when they break wind, which is often. There must be thirty of them at least, all armed with axes, swords, cudgels and morning stars. They come to a halt in the clearing, and their leader, a huge beast with a horned helmet and extra-long tusks, begins to bark out orders. Six Orc Scouts are sent off in different directions, with one of them coming straight towards you! If you want to draw your sword to strike the Orc as it passes by, turn to **4**. If you want to climb the tree to hide, turn to **204**.

70

You pull the gate open and walk up the path to the farmhouse with your nose twitching from the foul stench coming from the cabbages which are rotting in the field. The farmhouse itself is in a bad state of repair and all the windows are boarded up. There are two broken rocking chairs, a bucket and a pile of firewood on the front porch.

If you want to open the front door, turn to **28**. If you want to walk back to the entrance gate and head towards Kaad, turn to **307**.

You soon get used to sailing the *Blue Moon*, and with a calm sea and a good breeze, you make good headway. Snake Island is soon no more than a speck behind you on the horizon. The sun is shining brightly and feels good on your face. The *Blue Moon* carves its way gently through the blue waters, and you feel like there's nowhere else you'd rather be. Whilst enjoying the moment, you know that you need to make a plan and decide your destination. Should you sail east to Red River to escape from the assassins? Or should you sail back to Port Blacksand to confront Lord Azzur? Your thinking is interrupted when you see a large wooden ship sailing towards you from the east. As it draws closer, you see it has a single mast supporting a large square-rigged sail with cannons sticking out on both sides of the hull. A black flag on its stern confirms your fear that a pirate ship is heading your way. There is no way you can outrun the ship, and you have to think quickly how best to avoid being captured. If you want to let your mainsail go loose and lie down on the deck, pretending to be dead in the hope the pirates will have no interest in you, turn to **21**. If you want to jump into the sea and hide behind the boat, turn to **329**.

72

You are unable to keep your balance with the Giant Rat hanging on to your boot, and the barrel topples over, sending you tumbling to the ground. You are lying sprawled out in the rubbish when the crowd descends upon you. Two Guards take charge and grab your arms and another Guard takes your sword. Your feet are shackled, and you are dragged away to the cheers of the crowd. It's not long before you find yourself chained to a wall of a dark dungeon cell, awaiting the arrival of the Earl of Kaad who, you are told, will decide whether or not to hand you over to Lord Azzur. When he finally arrives, you can tell from the stern faces of Guards behind him that it is not good news. Your worst fears are confirmed when the Earl tells you solemnly that you will be taken in chains to Executioner's Square in Port Blacksand. Your adventure is over.

73

Three daggers fly past your head and sink harmlessly into the tavern wall. Not stopping to look back at the angry mob, you run through the tavern doorway and on down to the quayside. Turn to **234**.

74

The Seer invites you to sit down, and you notice there is a small wooden box in front of him on the table. "I know who you are," he says, fidgeting with a piece of bread. "No doubt you have a question for me? I should warn you that I only had one egg for breakfast today, so you can only ask me one question." If you want to ask him if he knows the whereabouts of Lord Azzur, turn to **208**. If you want to ask him to give you some information about the next assassin, turn to **257**.

75

You quickly rummage through your possessions and pull out the ancient scroll. Holding it in front of you with the Orcs bearing down on you, you try to remember the words to cast the spell. If you want to call out "I'm here, I'm there, but you don't know where", turn to **111**. If you want to call out "Now you see me, now you don't", turn to **394**.

76

The berries taste quite bitter, but you are hungry, and eat several handfuls of them. You set off again, and it isn't long before you begin to feel unwell. You lean against a tree and are violently ill. The red berries are poisonous. Lose 1 *SKILL* point. Roll 1 die and reduce your *STAMINA* by the number rolled. If you are still alive, turn to **242**.

Zeedle thanks you for the Gold Piece and tells you to sit down in the boat whilst he unties the rope. He pushes off and pulls hard on the oars, steering the boat towards the far bank whilst telling you tales about Baron Sukumvit and Fang. It's a warm day and he stops rowing briefly to drink some water from a leather flask and then offers it to you. Thirsty after the morning walk, you take a long swig of the cool water. By the time the boat reaches the other side of the river, you are suffering from a sharp pain in your stomach. Zeedle helps you out of the boat and asks if you are feeling all right. He helps you over to a bench, where you sit down, clutching your stomach. The pain intensifies, and you begin to sweat profusely. "It looks like the water isn't safe to drink around here," Zeedle says, sniggering. "I should tell you that I'm not the real ferryman. He's dead, I'm afraid. I only pretended to drink the water from the flask myself. I mean, who would want to swallow Devil Bug larvae? The pain you can feel is from the ravenous little bugs, which have hatched in your stomach. They are now eating their way out and it won't be long before they burst out. I'm afraid you are doomed. The moral of the story is never trust an Assassin!" You are paralysed by pain and you can only watch on helplessly as Zeedle reveals his scorpion pendant and dangles it in front of you with a sickly grin on his face. Your adventure is over.

78

You put the bottle to your lips and take a small sip of the cool liquid, which surprisingly tastes like apple juice. In fact, you are certain that it is apple juice and take another swig. Feeling no ill effects, you keep drinking until the bottle is empty. Add 1 *STAMINA* point. You can't help but burp, which wakes up the old man with a start. "Whoa!" he says, leaping to his feet. "Thief! Robber! Who are you? I'm just a simple apple grower. Don't draw your sword, I beg of you, don't draw your sword. I'm desperate and all I ask is that you pay me for my apple juice – I mean, my magic healing potion. A Gold Piece would be very generous of you, but a silver coin will do." If you want to give the man a coin, turn to **151**. If you want to draw your sword, turn to **301**.

79

You run over to the rope ladder, climb up it quickly and look down on the pirate crew to talk to them. As soon as you speak, they jeer you and call for you to walk the plank for killing their captain. One of them throws a dagger at you which strikes your leg. Lose 2 *STAMINA* points. A huge cheer goes up, and the others pull out their knives to do the same. You hold up your hand and tell them that you would rather walk the plank than be a target for their knife-throwing contest. Another cheer goes up, and you are escorted to the plank. You hear one of the pirates say, "With that bleeding leg, the Blood Sharks are going to be here in no time. I'll wager 5 Silver Pieces our friend here doesn't last ten minutes in the water! Any takers?" "Shut up and get on with it!" another says impatiently. You look out to sea, knowing you have to jump into the dangerous waters without much hope of survival. You breathe in deeply, step on the plank and take a running jump, hoping not to get sucked under the ship. You hear the pirates cheer loudly as you hit the water. When you surface, you swim as hard as you can towards the *Blue Moon* in tow. Roll two dice. If the number rolled is less than or equal to your *SKILL* score, turn to **265**. If the number rolled is greater than your *SKILL* score, turn to **144**.

80

You take careful aim at the man standing in the open window and release the arrow. Roll two dice. If the number rolled is less than or equal to your *SKILL* score, turn to **238**. If the number rolled is greater than your *SKILL* score, turn to **399**.

You are in considerable pain, lying in a pool of blood on the deck of the pirate ship. You open your eyes to a circle of pirate faces staring down at you. The captain pushes to the front of the circle and says, spitting with anger, "Nobody ever draws their sword on me and lives to tell the tale. But I'm not going to waste another bullet on you. It's the plank for you, matey!" The pirates cheer and lead you over to the gangplank, which is lashed amidships and hanging perilously out over the open sea. The pirates take all your possessions except for the few items in your pockets which they fail to notice in their ghoulish excitement. You are pushed on to the plank and one of the pirates says, "With that wound bleeding as it is, the Blood Sharks are going to be here in no time. I'll wager a Gold Piece our friend here doesn't last ten minutes in the water! Any takers?" "Shut up and get on with it!" one of the other pirates says impatiently. You look out to sea, fearful of having to jump into the dangerous waters without much hope of survival. You step on to the plank, breathe in deeply and take a running jump into the sea, hoping not to get sucked under the ship. You hear the pirates cheer loudly as you hit the water. When you surface, you swim as hard as you can towards the *Blue Moon* being towed along in the wake of the pirate ship. Roll two dice. If the number rolled is less than or equal to your *SKILL* score, turn to **265**. If the number rolled is greater than your *SKILL* score, turn to **144**.

82

There is a satisfying dull thud as the keen edge of your sword bites into the sinews and bones of the Dragon's left foot. The giant beast roars in pain and flaps its wings frantically, trying to lift itself back up into the sky. It flies off east, roaring loudly. You watch it shrink to a tiny speck on the horizon before sheathing your sword. You look around and see half of the Dragon's foot, which was sheared off by your sword, lying on the ground. Dragon claws command high prices in Port Blacksand, and you cut off two claws, hoping one day to sell them to an armourer to make exotic weapons. Pleased with your treasure, you head back towards your hut on the other side of the island. Turn to **217**.

83

You throw off your backpack without stopping (deduct all the possessions and Provisions in your backpack from your *Adventure Sheet*). You keep on running and soon come to the foot of a small hill. You run up and over the top to where you see a white-haired woman standing in a doorway which has been cut into the trunk of a huge oak tree. "Over here!" she cries, beckoning you over to her. "Quick, come inside and close the door behind you!" If you want to follow her through the doorway, turn to **63**. If you would rather keep on running, turn to **274**.

84

The innkeeper takes your knife and leans forward to whisper in your ear, saying, "You can see the poster behind me. I know who you are. I don't want any more dead bodies in my tavern. It's bad for business. Give me 5 Gold Pieces, walk casually out of the door and leave Port Blacksand while you can." If you want to give the innkeeper 5 Gold Pieces, turn to **110**. If you want to refuse to do so, turn to **253**.

85

You join the pirates in their struggle to lift the rowing boat over the side of the ship and into the sea, but the steep angle of the ship's deck makes it a near-impossible task. The boat is too heavy to hang on to, and the pirates are forced to let go of it. You watch it skid along the deck and smash into the wheelhouse, which makes a large hole in the rowing boat. The ship is now almost on its side, being dragged slowly underwater by the giant Kraken. Unable to stand up, you are forced to jump into the foaming sea with the rest of the crew. The ship creaks and splinters and begins to break up as it rolls upside down. You hear the unnerving bubbling sound of air escaping from the upturned hull as it is dragged underwater by the giant sea monster mixed with cries for help from pirates ensnared in the Kraken's tentacles. It is all you can do to stop yourself from being sucked underwater by the sinking ship. You swallow a lot of water and you feel your strength ebbing away. Lose 3 *STAMINA* points. All appears to be lost as you try to swim away from the carnage. Behind you, all that remains of the pirate ship are bits of rigging, broken planks, bottles and general flotsam. *Test Your Luck*. If you are Lucky, turn to **270**. If you are Unlucky, turn to **194**.

86

The woman throws back her cloak to show you that she is unarmed and says, "I won't take your distrust of me personally. I understand you can't be too careful in these parts! Let's shake hands and exchange tales." If you want to shake hands with the woman, turn to **313**. If you would rather draw your sword, turn to **35**.

87

You hear a rustling sound in the grass to the left of the path, followed by yelps and growls. The growls turn into the howls of a pack of four WOLVES which leap out in front of you. The lead Wolf is bigger than the others and its drooling jaw hangs open, displaying its sharp teeth. You step forward to attack the leader of the pack.

WOLF   SKILL 5   STAMINA 5

If you win, turn to **295**.

A gigantic tentacle rises out of the sea

88

You cut through the rope with one swipe of your sword and watch the pirate ship sail away. Moments later a gigantic tentacle rises out of the sea no more than twenty metres away from the pirate ship. Another tentacle rises out of the sea, then another, and another, until there are eight of them towering high in the sky. The ship is about to be attacked by a KRAKEN, a giant sea monster with a colossal squid-like body, two huge eyes and a beaked mouth. You hear booming explosions from the ship's cannon as two cannonballs whistle through the air towards the Kraken, one of them finding its mark and taking a big chunk out of one of the tentacles. The sea monster retaliates by wrapping two of its giant tentacles around the ship's mast. There is chaos on board when the Kraken starts pulling the ship over on to its side. Everything on deck that is not lashed down spills overboard. There is nothing the pirates can do to defeat the Kraken, and you hear them cry for help as they jump into the sea. You watch on in horror as the pirate ship rolls over and disappears below the waves, and the crew with it. Not wishing to be the Kraken's next victim, you hurriedly trim the *Blue Moon*'s flapping sail to get under way to escape from the sea monster. If you want to steer a course due east towards the Red River estuary, turn to **114**. If you want to sail south-east to Port Blacksand, turn to **310**.

"Hello stranger, you look lost."

89

You hurry along Clock Street, passing small shops and taverns. You see a noticeboard and recognize your face on the "Wanted" poster nailed to it. You keep your head down as you walk past merchants chatting in the street. You press on and look up briefly and see a man cross the street and walk towards you. He is wearing a long brown leather coat and a wide-brimmed brown leather hat pulled down low. He calls out to you, saying, "Hello, stranger, you look lost. I'm the town guide. Can I help you?" If you want to reply "Yes", turn to **31**. If you want to draw your sword, turn to **160**.

90

The boots help you run so fast that you are halfway down the path before the brothers see you. You keep on running at full speed and are almost at the gate before Bobby fires his blunderbuss at you. It's a long shot for such an unreliable weapon. Roll one die. If the number rolled is between 1 and 5, turn to **125**. If you roll a 6, turn to **323**.

91

The storekeeper thanks you for the Gold Piece and suggests you should consider buying some Provisions for your journey. If you want to buy Provisions, turn to **64**. If you want to ask him if he sells Elven Boots, turn to **317**.

92

Silence descends over the crowd. Azzur plays to the audience, rubbing his chin as though appearing to be deep in thought. "That's a good number," he says coldly. "But it's not good enough!" Turn to **25**.

93

Reacting with lightning-fast reflexes, you dodge left just in time as the Ninja's sharp blade splinters the top of the table. You draw your sword to fight the quick-footed Ninja, who is poised ready to strike again.

NINJA WARRIOR　　　　*SKILL 7*　　*STAMINA 6*

If you win, turn to **254**.

94

You keep on running and arrive at the foot of a small hill. Thankfully the Bag of Everything weighs practically nothing and without the burden of a heavy backpack you are able to run over the hill and down to a wooded area, where you see a silver-haired woman standing in a doorway which has been cut into the trunk of a huge oak tree. "Over here!" she cries, beckoning you over to her. "Quick, come inside and close the door behind you!" If you want to follow her through the doorway, turn to **63**. If you would rather keep on running, turn to **274**.

95

The pirate ship comes alongside the *Blue Moon* and you hear a gruff voice bark out an order. "One of you dogs jump on board the boat and toss the body in the sea. Tie a rope to the boat and we'll tow it to Port Blacksand and sell it." Your deception plan has failed. You open your eyes a fraction to see a scrawny-looking pirate standing on a plank above you, ready to dive into the sea. If you want to stand up and give yourself up to the pirates, turn to **290**. If you want to trim the sails of the *Blue Moon* and sail away from the pirate ship, turn to **361**.

96

There is not enough time to pick up and throw the spear before the warrior is upon you, wielding her long knives around furiously. She strikes you twice before you even draw your sword to defend yourself. Lose 4 *STAMINA* points. You stagger backwards and watch the wild-eyed warrior stand still for a second with her head tilted to one side before uttering her shrill war cry and attacking you again in a flurry of flashing blades.

ZENGIAN ULTRA   *SKILL 9*   *STAMINA 6*

If you win, turn to **22**.

97

You wipe the hideous slime off your sword and walk back to take a look inside the lair of the Decayer hidden in the undergrowth. It is nothing more than a circle of stones around a flattened piece of ground. You notice that one of the stones has been carved in the shape of an eye. If you want to pick it up, turn to **395**. If you would rather leave it where it is and head east, turn to **213**.

98

You walk into a small kitchen where a big man in a grubby apron is standing by a wooden bucket drinking water from a ladle. He looks friendly enough, but his face is flushed and sweat is pouring down his brow. His shirtsleeves are rolled up and you see his bulging forearms, which have come from hammering hot metal on an anvil most of his life. The blacksmith stops drinking and looks at you suspiciously with water trickling down his chin. "Don't you think you should knock before walking in here?" he says sternly. "What do you want?" If you want to reply that you wish to buy some horseshoes, turn to **20**. If you want to tell him that you are being hunted by assassins, turn to **371**.

99

Following the map, you leave the market square via a narrow alleyway to your left which leads into Spice Street, then turn right on to Boot Street, where you see a group of scruffy urchins throwing stones in a puddle. One of them runs over to you and says, "Do you want to buy a catapult? You can't miss with it. Only 1 Gold Piece. A bargain. Go on, buy it." If you want to buy the boy's catapult, turn to **181**. If you want to ignore him and walk on, turn to **261**.

100

The coin lands on the floor, and you hear soft footsteps followed by the dull sound of a blade slashing at your bedding several times. Whoever it is, they are trying their best to kill you in your sleep. If you want to swing your sword in the direction of the intruder, turn to **315**. If you want to run outside, turn to **124**.

101

The sweeping plain is tall grassland as far as you can see, all the way to the forest in the dim distance. The path cuts straight through the long grasses, which sway slowly from side to side in the gentle breeze. Walking along, you see a pair of legs sticking out of the grass up ahead and an open backpack next to them. Whoever it is, they are groaning loudly and appear to be in a lot of pain. You draw your sword and approach cautiously. If you want to investigate, turn to **173**. If you want to ignore the person and keep walking along the path, turn to **363**.

102

The man eyes you up and down, looking at you as though he knows you from somewhere. He purses his lips, shakes his head slowly and says, "No, I don't recall meeting anybody called Vassell. Mind you, your face looks familiar, but I just can't place it." You decide to change the subject. Will you:

Ask the man if he's interested in buying a boat?	Turn to **380**
Wish him farewell and go to the general store?	Turn to **327**
Wish him farewell and set off east on foot?	Turn to **203**

103

You slump back against the cellar wall, breathing hard, tired out after the hard-fought close combat. The brothers start clapping and cheering. "That was some fight, stranger. You sure gave Dax the Axe a lesson in swordplay all right, and the double-crossing skunk deserved it!" You ignore the brothers and pull back the Barbarian's cloak to find a silver necklace with a scorpion pendant. You break the chain and pocket the pendant, and curse Lord Azzur. You take two emerald rings from the Barbarian's left hand and open his leather pouch to find 18 Gold Pieces. "That's a fine haul, but you will have to make us an offer we can't refuse if you want us to let you go," Bobby says, pointing his blunderbuss at you. If you want to offer the brothers an axe, an emerald ring and half the Gold Pieces, turn to **10**. If you want to offer both axes, both rings and all the Gold Pieces, turn to **191**.

104

The water around you is blood-red. The Sea Snake's lifeless body floats slowly away on the current, leaving you free to swim over to the barrel. It is an old oak cask which is secured to the sea bed by a rusty chain. You are unable to remove the chain from the barrel but are able to prise off the wooden lid with your knife. You see a bronze shield, verdigris in colour, lying in a few inches of water at the bottom of the barrel. If you want to swim back to the shore with the shield, turn to **9**. If you would rather swim back to shore without the shield, gather up your belongings, and climb back up the stone steps to the top of the cliff, turn to **127**.

105

The storekeeper hands you the food, which will add 4 *STAMINA* points when eaten. You thank the storekeeper and decide what to do next. If you want to ask him if he has heard of Garanka Vassell, turn to **229**. If you want to leave the store and head east on foot, turn to **203**.

A long-haired Barbarian wearing an eyepatch

106

Weakened by your wounds, you sink to your knees under the weight of the Berserker's ferocious blows. You wonder how much more of the relentless onslaught you can take when you suddenly notice a long-haired Barbarian wearing an eyepatch running towards you from the town gates armed with two throwing axes. When he is no more than ten metres away, he hurls one of his axes at the Berserker and you hear it sink into his back with a dull thud. He immediately throws the second axe, which also strikes home. The Berserker teeters for a moment before toppling forward to land on top of you. You are pinned down by the dead weight of the body, unable to move. You watch the Barbarian walk up to retrieve his axes and are relieved to see that he is not wearing a silver necklace. His stern look turns into a half smile, and he drags the dead body off you and helps you to your feet. After thanking the Barbarian for saving your life, you snatch the silver scorpion from the Berserker's neck and place it in your pocket. The Barbarian introduces himself as Throm and tells you that Urzle Ironface was a slave pit fighter who gained his freedom after killing a hundred opponents, one of whom was Throm's brother. Throm asks why the Berserker tried to kill you and you tell him about the multiple assassination attempts on your life and that you have come to Fang to find Lord Azzur and settle the issue. Throm slaps you on the back and says, "That's bold!

I'm here for the Trial of Champions. It begins tomorrow. If you enter the contest, you'll be introduced to the Baron and Lord Azzur. It's probably your best chance of getting close to him. There's still time to enter if you want to?" You agree to Throm's plan and gather up your belongings. Certain that Lord Azzur will have put his "Wanted" posters up around town, you decide to wear Urzle Ironface's face-covering iron helmet so that nobody will recognize you when you enter Fang. Turn to **309**.

107

A crossbow bolt sinks into the back of your leg with a dull thud. Lose 2 *STAMINA* points. The pain in your back is terrible when you pull the bolt out, but there is no time to treat the wound, as the tavern door bursts open. A bald-headed man wearing a chain mail vest storms out of the tavern screaming, and charges at you like a raging bull, swinging a two-handed sword above his head. You notice that he has a dent in his skull and all his teeth are made of gold. It is the deadly assassin Garanka Vassell and you must fight him. Turn to **53**.

108

Your attempt to swat the bees is futile and they continue to sting you relentlessly. Lose 2 *STAMINA* points. You have no choice but to climb down the tree as fast as you can. Turn to **336**.

109

You look down at the assassin and see a silver necklace around his neck with the familiar scorpion pendant hanging off it. You snap the chain and put the pendant in your pocket as a crowd forms around you, whispering among themselves about the body on the ground. The mood of the crowd darkens, and an old man calls out to you accusingly, demanding to know who started the fight. You feel a tug on your shirt and look round to see a young woman in a long, hooded red cloak. She has piercing green eyes and she looks very anxious. "Quick, follow me before they realize who you are!" she whispers urgently in your ear. "There are posters everywhere with your face on them!" If you want to follow the woman, turn to **293**. If you want to run back the way you came, turn to **314**.

110

Trying not to attract attention, you take 5 Gold Pieces out of your pocket and slide them over to the innkeeper, who gives you a slight nod of the head in acknowledgement. You watch him tap a bottle loudly with a spoon and call for silence in the tavern. "The next round is on me!" he shouts out to his customers, who respond with a loud cheer. They all rush to the bar, giving you the chance to slip out of the tavern unnoticed. You make your way quickly down to the quay to where the *Blue Moon* is, thankfully, still moored. Leaning against the bollard is an unshaven, one-armed beggar with his head bowed. His dirty, baggy shirt and ragged cotton pants are partially covered by a moth-eaten blanket. He rattles a tin mug at you and says in a quivering voice, "Spare me a coin and I'll untie your boat for you." If you want to give the beggar a coin to help you cast off, turn to **389**. If you want to ignore him and untie the mooring rope yourself and jump on board your boat, turn to **129**.

111

You blurt out the words, but nothing happens. You are still visible to the band of screaming Orcs, which crashes into you with the force of a herd of stampeding Hippohogs.

Their flailing swords, axes, morning stars and cudgels make light work of your pitiful resistance, and the battle lasts less than a minute. Your adventure is over.

112

You manage to steady yourself and watch the loose step roll down the cliff face on to the beach below. You tread carefully the rest of the way down, reach the beach without further mishap and walk over to the cave entrance. Turn to **201**.

113

You throw the Gold Pieces up in the air, which causes a huge commotion behind you. The townsfolk stop giving chase and pile on top of each other on the ground in a mad scramble to snatch one of the coins for themselves. You don't stop to look back and turn right into Fountain Street and run in the Public Gardens up ahead on the left to hide. Turn to **268**.

114

Apart from Blood Sharks circling you at one point, the voyage to the mainland passes without incident. A strong easterly breeze speeds up the journey, and a few hours later the rugged Allansian coastline comes into view. The cliffs are quite high, but you see an estuary directly ahead which you know to be the entrance to Red River. It's not long before you are at the mouth of the river, where you see two wooden buildings on the northern bank. You steer the *Blue Moon* over to the bank, jump out, and tie it up to a small dock. It feels good to be back on dry land, but you are also very aware that Lord Azzur will not rest until one of his assassins has delivered your head to him. If only Captain Crow had told you who the other assassins were before he died, you would be better prepared. Now you suspect everybody you meet could be one of Azzur's assassins. But at least you should recognize Garanka Vassell when you see him, if not the other assassins. You walk towards the buildings, which you see are a boatyard and a general store. Thinking you might be able to get some gold by selling the *Blue Moon*, you decide to visit the boatyard first. Turn to **288**.

115

Frightened by your presence, the chicks don't stop screeching, and suddenly you hear the Orc calling from below. You look down and see the ugly brute at the base of the tree staring up at you, gesturing for you to come down.

If you want to climb down to fight him, turn to **235**. If you want to stay where you are, turn to **286**.

116

Picking your way through the thick undergrowth, you see a tall bush with lots of ripe red berries hanging from its branches. If you want to eat the berries, turn to **76**. If you would rather walk on, turn to **242**.

117

The Monk's eyes light up when you produce the 5 Gold Pieces. He rummages around in his sack and hands you a rolled-up piece of yellowed paper tied with a piece of string. After taking the coins from you, he rubs his hands together with glee and says:

> "Five Gold Pieces, my oh my
> Think of all the cheese I'll buy
> Thanks again and I wish you well
> Especially at the Wishing Well!"

He picks up his sack, throws it over his shoulder and walks off at a brisk pace. You untie the string and unroll the paper scroll and see that it is a map, but not one which requires you to travel very far. The Wishing Well is marked with an "X" in the Public Gardens in Fountain Street in Kaad! You are annoyed with yourself for paying so much for the map and wonder if it will be worthwhile going to the well. If you want to follow the map to Fountain Street, turn to **99**. If you want to walk across the market square to Clock Street, turn to **140**.

118

You tentatively place the headband on, keeping both hands on it just in case you need to pull it off again. You wait for a minute, but nothing happens. Feeling no ill effects, you think about what to do. If you want to look at the books on the bookshelves, turn to **355**. If you want to walk up the stairs and go back outside, turn to **305**.

119

You take aim and hurl the meat cleaver at the pirate as hard as you can but are disheartened as you watch it fly over his head and land harmlessly in the sea. The scraggy pirate laughs at you and waves goodbye, sailing the *Blue Moon* east towards the mainland. Behind you, all that remains of the pirate ship is some rigging, bits of broken wood, and miscellaneous deck gear. *Test Your Luck*. If you are Lucky, turn to **270**. If you are Unlucky, turn to **194**.

120

The woman signals for her driver to stop, and he pulls on his reins to bring his horse to a halt. He sits there rigidly, staring straight ahead with his long whip and reins in his hands. The woman looks down at you from her bench seat and says in a haughty voice, "I recognize you from the posters in town. I was at a banquet last night as a guest of Lord Azzur, who was in Kaad for the day. He's a loathsome tyrant and I don't believe a word he says, but he claimed that you murdered his master. You don't look like a murderer to me. If you were hoping to find Azzur in Kaad, I'm afraid you are going to be disappointed. He left this morning for Fang. He's gone to see his old friend Baron Sukumvit, who is holding his annual Trial of Champions. Did you know that nobody has ever come out of Deathtrap Dungeon alive? Quite astonishing really. But there is always some fool who is willing to give it a go! Anyway, I must be on my way. I can offer you a ride as far as Otto's Outpost on the Pagan Plains if that is of interest?" If you want to accept the woman's offer, turn to **14**. If you want to enter the gates of Kaad, turn to **243**.

121

You continue your journey north and enter another wooded area. Not long after entering the woods, you hear the sound of marching feet coming from the east and deep voices singing a very rude song about the Dwarfs of Stonebridge. If you want to stand behind a tree and wait to see who is about to enter the clearing ahead, turn to **69**. If you would rather hurry on north, turn to **263**.

122

You lift the lid to find a small iron key with the number 44 stamped on it. You see it is a skeleton key which will open most locks. Add 1 *LUCK* point. Pleased with your find, you pocket the key and look around the cave. Turn to **365**.

123

You walk quickly up Bell Street without looking back and turn left into Fountain Street, where you see the town's Public Gardens up ahead on the right. Turn to **268**.

124

The intruder hears your footsteps and swings his long knife in your direction, slicing your arm with the tip of the blade. Lose 2 *STAMINA* points. You turn to defend yourself and must fight the agile KNIFE FIGHTER in total darkness!

KNIFE FIGHTER   SKILL 7   STAMINA 8

If you win, turn to **174**.

125

You hear a loud bang behind you and see a clump of cabbages to your left get shredded by lead shot. Seconds later you reach the farmhouse gate and turn around to see the twins sitting on the roof with Bobby holding his blunderbuss in the air, a wisp of white smoke drifting out of the barrel. They give you the thumbs up and call out to congratulate you. Add 1 *LUCK* point. They start waving and laughing so hard that they almost fall off the roof. You decide it best to leave them to it and bandage your leg before heading for Kaad. Turn to **307**.

126

The assassin holds out her hand and when you shake it, a violent pain shoots up your arm. Her face immediately lights up with evil glee, and she starts laughing hysterically. You try to pull your hand away but are unable to do so. Your hands are locked together in a cloud of swirling green mist which grows in size as the pain increases and spreads into your chest. Lose 2 *STAMINA* points. "What a gullible fool you are," she sneers. "Never trust an assassin! The pain you are experiencing will, I regret to say, lead to your heart stopping in a minute. Tonight, I will return to Port Blacksand with your head and claim the bounty of 1,000 Gold Pieces from Lord Azzur." If you were harmed by the Hand of Death on Snake Island, turn to **146**. If you didn't touch the Hand of Death, turn to **379**.

A Fire Dragon swooping down to land

127

You are about to head back to your hut on the other side of the island when you hear a loud roar above you like the sound of flames being fanned by giant bellows. You look up to see a FIRE DRAGON swooping down to land in the open space where you are standing. If you want to run for cover, turn to **391**. If you want to stand your ground and fight the giant fire-breathing creature, turn to **289**.

128

You do not have to wait long before somebody comes to your rescue. A long-haired man wearing animal skins and brown pants suddenly appears in front of you. He is carrying a wooden staff and a large canvas bag over his shoulder. He looks disappointed to see you and says, "You are not what I was hoping to catch in my trap! I suppose I'm going to have to set you free, but it's going to cost you." He holds out his hand expectantly and asks for 1 Gold Piece for his troubles. After you pay him, he takes a small key from his pocket and unlocks the trap. He helps you to your feet and trudges off to inspect his other traps. You bandage your swollen ankle and return to the path, eventually coming to a rickety old gate on the right which has a large sign nailed to it with the words BOGG FARM – BOG OFF painted on it. A gravel path leads from the gate to an old farmhouse, which sits in the middle of a small field separated from the grassland by a wooden fence. There is a stone post next to the gate with an arrow carved on it, pointing towards the town, and the words KAAD – 1 MILE underneath. From this distance, Kaad looks like it is a small town. The buildings are few in number and are mostly one or two storeys high except a stone tower in the centre of town. If you want to open the gate and walk up the path to the farmhouse, turn to **70**. If you would rather continue on to Kaad, turn to **307**.

129

You yell at the beggar to move out of the way so that you can untie the boat from its mooring. As you reach for the rope, he suddenly throws off his blanket to reveal a sword held in the hand you thought was missing! With steely-cold eyes and a sinister smile, he lunges at you with his sword from close range, and wounds you badly in the midriff. Lose 1 *SKILL* point and 4 *STAMINA* points. If you are still alive, you must do what you can to defend yourself against the ELITE SWORDSMAN who lunges forward to strike you again.

ELITE SWORDSMAN   *SKILL 8*   *STAMINA 5*

If you win, turn to **190**.

130

You are about to pass out but manage to put your lips to the Warp Ring and suddenly feel like you are tumbling head over heels through a black void with lights flashing in your head. You hear a loud bang and wake to find yourself standing in front of the gold podium, where Baron Sukumvit is standing next to Lord Azzur, surrounded by his elite Guards. You have gone back in time and decide with a second chance to show restraint and wait to be introduced to Baron Sukumvit. Turn to **233**.

131

A thick glob of drool hits your neck and starts to burn your skin like acid. The pain is intense, and you frantically pour water from your water bottle on to the open wound to stop the drool burning deeper into your skin. Lose 1 *SKILL* point and 2 *STAMINA* points. The Decayer lumbers towards you and you have no choice but to fight it. Turn to **306**.

132

Your powerful punch knocks Zeedle over and he lands on his back on the jetty. You pounce on him before he can sit up, pinning him down with your knees. You pull down the neck of his jumper and see the all-too-familiar scorpion pendant, which you snatch from its silver chain. Zeedle looks at you defiantly and spits out a tooth from his bloodied mouth. "You can't win," he says, grinning, trying to distract you as he reaches for a dagger hidden in his boot. Sensing his move, you punch him again and push him into the river. He lands with a splash and begins swimming frantically towards the bank. Attracted by the blood from his mouth, a school of SNAPPERFISH race in to attack him. A look of terror grips his face. He screams and spins round and round as the carnivorous fish begin their feeding frenzy, churning up the blood-red water. It's all over in seconds. You step aboard the boat and row yourself across the river to the opposite bank, wondering what fate awaits you in Fang. Turn to **163.**

133

The path takes you north through woods and open countryside on a walk which you would be enjoying more if you were not constantly looking over your shoulder for would-be assassins. Ahead you see a small man sitting cross-legged on an old moss-covered bench made of oak. He is a GNOME with a long, pointed nose, long grey beard and long grey hair poking out from under his floppy green hat. He is wearing a bottle-green tunic and leggings and a pair of old leather boots which you notice have big holes in the soles. He looks at you with a sleepy expression on his face as he chews slowly on a piece of straw. "You don't by chance have a pair of boots for sale, do you?" he asks nonchalantly as you pass by. "Mine have had it and my feet are killing me. I'm willing to pay 1 Gold Piece for a pair of leather boots. And I'd gladly pay 10 Gold Pieces for a pair of Elven Boots." If you have a spare pair of boots that you wish to sell, turn to **32**. If you would rather carry on walking north, turn to **179**.

134

There are two pirates standing on the stern of the ship, and one of them spots you climbing on board the *Blue Moon*. He sounds the alarm, and more pirates run to the stern to find out what is going on. The captain appears on deck, pistol in hand, wearing a bright burgundy coat with brass buttons, and a matching coloured hat with a white plume. He takes aim at you with his pistol and pulls the trigger. There is a loud bang and a puff of white smoke. *Test Your Luck*. If you are Lucky, turn to **198**. If you are Unlucky, turn to **245**.

135

You walk briskly west until you come to a junction in the path where it meets another path running north-south. You don't see any point in going back south so you turn right and head north towards the forest, which you can see in the distance. Turn to **87**.

136

You tell the man about the tragic events that led to Captain Crow's death. He shakes his head and says, "Well, Sam didn't have no family, so I guess it's all right for you to sell his boat. But I'm not going to give you much for it mind, just in case you are making this story up. I'll give you 20 Gold Pieces for her, take it or leave it." If you want to accept his offer, turn to **375**. If you want to demand 30 Gold Pieces for the boat, turn to **29**.

137

Brick Street ends at a junction of Boot Street and Quiet Street. There are some mischievous-looking urchins in Boot Street, so you decide to turn right into Quiet Street where, strangely, all the people are tiptoeing along in bare feet with their shoes tucked under their arms. Everybody is communicating by gesture and nobody is making a sound. An old woman wearing a headscarf looks at you fiercely and puts her index finger to her lips and points at your boots. If you want to take off your boots, turn to **335**. If you want to keep them on, turn to **360**.

138

You are unable to get out of the way of the Flesh-Head, which barrels into you, sending you tumbling over the cliff edge to the beach below. *Test Your Luck*. If you are Lucky, turn to **388**. If you are Unlucky, turn to **66**.

139

You put on your backpack and are about to set off when you suddenly feel a sharp, stabbing pain in your neck. You reach up and feel something smooth writhing in your fingers. It is a tiny gold-coloured snake which has injected you with poison. Lose 2 *STAMINA* points. You realize that the gold armband must be a deadly Mamba Band which comes alive unless worn. You throw the snake on to the ground and cleave it in two with your sword. Not wishing to chance it coming alive again, you kick it into the long grass. You tend to your wound whilst deciding which way to go next. If you want to keep going north, turn to **87**. If you want to head east along the new path, turn to **222**.

140

There is a Clock Tower in Clock Street set back on the right-hand side in the middle of a large paved area where a few townsfolk are sitting on benches, busily chatting to each other. The tall stone tower has a square base and has a clock face on each of its four sides at the top. You notice that the hands of one of the clocks are missing. There is a brass plaque by the front door of the tower with the name Balthazar Wittle inscribed on it. If you want to knock on the door, turn to **249**. If you want to carry on walking down Clock Street, turn to **89**.

141

The pirate told the truth. The Snakefang earring acts as an antidote to the toxic snake venom and you are unharmed by the dart. You draw your sword and rush forward to fight Tunku Yang, the notorious Poisoner of Kay-Pong. He looks surprised that you have survived his poisoned dart, and lunges at you armed with only a dagger.

TUNKU YANG   *SKILL 5*   *STAMINA 6*

If you lose an *Attack Round*, turn to **59**. If you win without losing an *Attack Round*, turn to **326**.

142

After a short tussle, you land a large eel on the rock where you are standing. It is brightly coloured, with vivid green and purple stripes running the length of its body. It has a long head with black eyes and a mouth with bulbous red lips and protruding needle-like teeth. It thrashes around on the rock, frantically trying to unhook itself from your line, and touches your leg with its tail. You suddenly feel a sharp pain run up your leg. You have been stung by an ELECTRO EEL. Lose 1 *SKILL* point and 1 *STAMINA* point. You stagger backwards in shock as the eel slips off its hook and slithers back into the sea. Lose 1 *LUCK* point. You decide you have had enough of fishing for the day and head inland in search of food. Turn to **116**.

143

"Well, give us 3 Gold Pieces and you can have it and be on your way! Brother Bobby made it himself, he did. Carved the little piggy out of a piece of wood and painted it gold. Looks just like the real thing, don't it?" Billy says, slapping his thigh and laughing like a neighing donkey. If you have 3 Gold Pieces and wish to buy the painted carving, turn to **67**. If you don't have 3 Gold Pieces or don't want to buy the carving, turn to **381**.

144

You do not have enough strength left to swim to the *Blue Moon* before the Blood Sharks swim in to attack. Your struggle against them is brief before the feeding frenzy begins. Your adventure is over.

145

As soon as he sees your face, Lord Azzur points at you and shouts, "It's the murderer!" Baron Sukumvit orders his

Guards to arrest you. "No, not yet!" Azzur says sharply. "I admire the nerve of this fool. I want to know how many of my assassins have been killed." You remain silent and take the scorpion pendants out of your pocket and rattle them in your hand. "So, you think this is a game, do you?" Azzur continues in his sneering voice. "Right, let's play your game. Tell me, do you have an odd number or an even number of pendants in your hand?" If you want to reply "Odd", turn to **259**. If you want to reply "Even", turn to **25**.

146

Thanks to your encounter with the Hand of Death on Snake Island, your body has built up some immunity to Death Hand magic. Add 1 *LUCK* point. You are still in agony, but the pain is bearable enough for you to be able to draw a knife from your belt with your free hand. You slice open the back of the assassin's hand, forcing her to release her grip. She curses and pulls out two short swords from sheaths hidden behind her back. You draw your sword and advance to fight the wounded assassin.

GRETTA MORG   *SKILL 8*   *STAMINA 5*

If you win, turn to **321**.

A quick glance left solves the mystery

147

You manage to trace your path back to the beach on the west side of Snake Island and are quite relieved to see your hut again. You are about to go inside when you see a boat moored up on the beach. It's the *Blue Moon*, the same boat that brought you to the island. Captain Crow is on board, standing on deck. He looks anxious when you approach him but says nothing. When you call out to him, he doesn't reply, but his eyes dart right several times, as though he is trying to warn you about something. A quick glance left solves the mystery. Crouched down in the shadows of a large rock is a hooded figure in leather armour holding a loaded bow aimed straight at you. You hear a faint twang as the arrow is released from the bow. If you are carrying a shield, turn to **13**. If you do not have a shield, turn to **312**.

148

You have stepped on an animal trap. The jagged iron jaws snap shut on your left ankle and bite into the bone. Lose 2 *STAMINA* points. You discover that the trap is chained to a large rock buried in the ground. Unable to escape, you try prising the jaws apart with your sword, but the spring holding them shut is too strong. You notice there is a small keyhole on the base of the trap. If you have a small iron skeleton key, turn to the number which is stamped on it. If you do not have this key, turn to **397**.

149

The barmaid takes one look at you and shrieks loudly, dropping one of her mugs of ale. Everybody in the tavern turns towards you. Several rough-looking villains stand up, daggers in hand. "It's the murderer!" one of them cries. "It's more like 1,000 Gold Pieces on legs!" an old pickpocket shouts excitedly. Surrounded by the noisy mob, you decide to run for it. You kick over the table in front of you and dash for the door. Although the crowd is distracted by the flying table, three thieves still manage to throw their daggers at you. *Test Your Luck*. If you are Lucky, turn to **73**. If you are Unlucky, turn to **225**.

150

You run down the alleyway, which comes to a dead end at a high wall where two GIANT RATS are scavenging through a pile of rubbish which has been dumped against the wall. If you want to try to climb over the wall, turn to **320**. If you want to turn around to face the angry crowd, turn to **352**.

151

The man gives you a big hug when you pay him and thanks you over and over again. He reaches into his pocket and produces a clover leaf charm. "Please take this with my compliments," he says, smiling, handing you the small charm. "It was carved out of Salamonian goat horn. It will bring you good luck on your travels." You take it from him and put it in your pocket. Add 2 *LUCK* points. You shake the man's hand and bid him farewell before setting off east again. Turn to **277**.

152

You keep your head down as you climb back on board the *Blue Moon*, very aware that lots of bad people will be looking for you to claim Azzur's reward. You cast off, setting a northerly course towards Red River. Apart from the boat being rocked by a school of Blubber Whales swimming close by, the voyage passes without incident. You sail along the rugged Allansian coastline until you come to an estuary which you know to be the entrance to Red River. You sail a short distance up the river to see two wooden buildings on the northern bank. You steer the *Blue Moon* over to the bank, jump out, and tie it up to a small dock. It feels good to be back on dry land, but you are also very aware that Lord Azzur will not rest until one of his assassins has delivered your head to him. If only Captain Crow had told you who the other assassins were before he died, you would be better prepared. Now everybody you meet could be one of Azzur's assassins. But at least you should recognize Garanka Vassell when you see him. You walk towards the buildings, which you note are a boatyard and a general store. Thinking you might be able to sell the *Blue Moon*, you decide to visit the boatyard first. Turn to **288**.

153

You pay the horseman 2 Gold Pieces and are soon galloping across the open plain. You soon discover that he is not keen to talk, and the only question he answers is when you ask him where he is going. "Firetop Mountain," he replies curtly, but doesn't elaborate when you ask him why. As the light fades you hear the howls and growls of the creatures of the night, which are eager to begin their hunt for food. By the time you arrive at the log cabin, shadows are already creeping over the plain. "This is where you get off," the horseman says abruptly, pointing towards the cabin. You jump down from his horse and watch him gallop off without another word said. The log cabin looks to be well built and secured with wooden shutters on all the windows. There is a wooden sign above the door which reads OTTO'S OUTPOST. It's been a grisly day and you are looking forward to a good night's sleep. Turn to **264**.

154

The lightning strikes the wooden mast, causing the mainsail to catch fire. Without a sail there is nothing the captain can do to steer the crippled craft. The storm continues to rage, and the captain loses control of the boat. A rogue wave crashes over the deck and washes you both overboard. Swimming in the heavy seas is exhausting, and by the time the dreaded Blood Sharks begin to circle, you have no strength left to fight them. Your adventure is over.

155

Zeedle watches on in disbelief as you wade into the river. Something brushes against your leg and suddenly the water churns up all around you. You feel a bite on your leg, swiftly followed by another, then another. The blood seeping from your cuts and wounds has attracted a school of SNAPPERFISH. Your blood runs freely, which sends the carnivorous fish into a feeding frenzy. The last thing you see is Zeedle rowing frantically over to you with a smile on his face and a dagger between his teeth. Your adventure is over.

156

The intruder's dagger just misses your head and thuds into the wall behind you. You retaliate by swiping your sword through the darkness, and feel it strike home. A man's muffled cry breaks the silence, and you hear him stumble backwards. You step forward to finish off the intruder, who is a skilful KNIFE FIGHTER. Although injured, he is agile and quick on his feet, and you must fight him in total darkness.

KNIFE FIGHTER   *SKILL 7*   *STAMINA 6*

If you win, turn to **174**.

157

You leave the tavern behind and ten minutes later you see a rickety-looking wooden table to the left of the path which is piled high with apples. There is a handwritten sign nailed to the table which says FREE APPLES. HELP YOURSELF. If you would like to eat an apple, turn to **221**. If you would rather keep heading east, turn to **358**.

158

The pain in your head steadily increases to the point that you pass out. Alas, you never wake up, and the next day Red Ruth rides to Port Blacksand to collect the reward of 1,000 Gold Pieces from Lord Azzur. Your adventure is over.

159

With supreme effort, you manage to prise one of the fingers away from your throat and snap it off. A wisp of green smoke escapes from the hollow of the broken finger, forming a small cloud in which the outline of the grinning face of an evil spirit appears. If you want to continue trying to prise the other fingers away from your throat, turn to **299**. If you want to take a swipe at the smoke cloud, turn to **188**.

160

The man curses and draws a sabre from his belt, shouting, "I, Blackthorn of Chalice, will see your head delivered to Lord Azzur." He runs at you with his sabre raised in the air.

BLACKTHORN   *SKILL 8*   *STAMINA 7*

If you win, turn to **109**.

161

As you open the door, you are stabbed in the arm by the intruder. Lose 2 *STAMINA* points. Unable to see your attacker, you swing your sword blindly in the pitch-black darkness and feel it strike home. A man's muffled cry breaks the silence. The intruder is a skilful KNIFE FIGHTER, quick-witted and agile, and you must fight him in the dark.

KNIFE FIGHTER   *SKILL 7*   *STAMINA 6*

If you win, turn to **174**.

162

The men's eyes light up when they hear your offer to buy their fish. The fisherman who claimed to have caught all the fish picks up the bucket and thrusts it at you, which makes water slosh over the sides. There are six fish in the bucket and the man says he'll include the bucket for the price. You hand him a Gold Piece, which brings a big smile to his face. The men gather up their fishing equipment and head off west, and start arguing again, this time about the Gold Piece. You ignore them and set about making a fire and you are soon tucking into tasty grilled fish. Add 2 *STAMINA* points. Feeling content and well fed, you head north to walk along the bank of the tributary. Turn to **47**.

"I am the berserker, Urzle Ironface."

163

After tying the rowing boat to a wooden jetty, you walk along a cart track towards Fang in good spirits, heartened by the knowledge that Lord Azzur can't be far away. As you approach the main gates, a giant bare-chested man with bulging muscles steps out from behind the jail to stand in your way. His body is covered in jagged scars, and he makes no attempt to hide the silver scorpion pendant hanging on a silver necklace around his neck. He is wearing an iron helmet which completely covers his face and he is armed with a large battle-axe and shield. "I've been waiting for you," he growls slowly in a deep voice. "I knew you would come. You have defeated many assassins. But you cannot defeat me. I am the ultimate assassin. I am the berserker, Urzle Ironface. There is a bounty is on your head and I must do what must be done. It cannot be undone. This is my pledge to Lord Azzur." The huge man smashes his axe against his shield and strides forward to attack you.

URZLE IRONFACE   SKILL 12   STAMINA 12

If you are still alive after 5 Attack Rounds, turn to **247**.

164

The woman looks slightly off balance when you ask her the question. "No, I'm afraid not. Why do you ask?" she replies, composing herself again. You suddenly catch sight of a necklace which was previously concealed by her hood. It looks to be made of silver. You take two steps backwards with your hand on the hilt of your sword. She looks at you aghast, and says, "Please refrain from drawing your sword. If you think I am an assassin, you are most certainly wrong. As you can see I am not carrying a sword and, apart from my arrows and whittling knife, I am completely unarmed." If you want to pull back her cloak so you can see if she is hiding a weapon, turn to **86**. If you want to attack her with your sword, turn to **287**.

165

The Dragon is covered with red, iron-like scales which look too thick to penetrate with your sword, so you aim your blow at its clawed feet, which are just above your head. Roll two dice. If the total is equal to or less than your *SKILL* score, turn to **82**. If the number is greater than your *SKILL* score, turn to **262**.

166

You become aware of a faint smell of smoke in the air and look round to see a thick plume of black smoke rising above the treetops into the sky. Whilst you are watching the smoke rise, you do not notice the window open on the first floor of the tavern and a crossbow appear which is aimed at you. Roll one die. If you roll a 1 or a 2, turn to **269**. If you roll a 3 or a 4, turn to **107**. If you roll a 5 or a 6, turn to **62**.

167

Balthazar shakes his head and says, "No, I'm glad I haven't seen that despicable tyrant, and you are going to be disappointed if you were hoping to find him in Kaad. He held a banquet here last night for his cronies, and I heard he left this morning for Fang. He's gone to see his friend Baron Sukumvit, who is holding his annual Trial of Champions. Anyway, I have to get back to my work, so I'm going to say goodbye." Balthazar shuts the door, leaving you no option but to walk further up Clock Street. Turn to **89**.

168

You hear gasps of disbelief from the crew as you move to draw your sword, but the captain simply sneers and pulls the trigger of his pistol. *Test Your Luck*. If you are Lucky, turn to **52**. If you are Unlucky, turn to **350**.

169

The warrior's aim is deadly accurate. Her spear pierces your armour and lodges in your shoulder. Lose 2 *STAMINA* points. You manage to yank it free with the warrior closing in fast wielding two long knives. You draw your sword and ready yourself for combat. Turn to **266**.

170

The storekeeper rummages through all his drawers without success but finds a pair of boots under a pile of sacks on one of the top shelves. "I knew I had a pair somewhere," he says to himself with satisfaction, dusting them off. "They're not new, but they were made by a High Elf master boot-maker. Look at the quality of the leather and the stitching. If you wear these, you will be able to outrun anybody. I'm loath to sell my last pair, but I'll let you have them for 5 Gold Pieces." Will you:

Buy the boots?	Turn to **351**
Reject the boots and buy some Provisions?	Turn to **64**
Leave the store and head east on foot?	Turn to **203**

171

Silence descends over the crowd. Azzur plays to the audience, rubbing his chin as though appearing to be deep in thought. "That's a good number," he says coldly. "But it's not good enough!" Turn to **25**.

172

You are caught by a blast of flame. Lose 2 *SKILL* points and 4 *STAMINA* points. The burning pain is intense, but you dare not stop running. With its giant leathery wings flapping noisily above you, the Dragon climbs into the sky, ready to swoop down to attack you again with its fiery breath. Running into the undergrowth, you are quick to spot an entrance to a burrow in the ground, perhaps a den made by a wild animal. If you want to jump down feet first into the burrow to hide from the Dragon, turn to **285**. If you want to keep on running, turn to **325**.

173

You part the tall grass with your sword and see a man dressed in green-and-brown woodsman's clothing lying face down with a dagger sticking out of his back. He groans loudly when you turn him on his side. "It's too late for me," he whispers slowly, staring at you with unblinking eyes. "Two Hobgoblins jumped me. I fought them off, but there was another one hiding in the long grass who stabbed me in the back. They took everything I had and left me for dead." The man grimaces in pain and breathes in hard before carrying on. "The cowardly dogs missed my gold. Take it." The man's eyes suddenly widen, and he goes listless. There is nothing you can do to save the woodsman. You find a hidden pocket in the seam of his tunic containing 3 Gold Pieces which you place in your pocket and continue your journey. Turn to **363**.

174

Breathing hard after the desperate fight, you think about who your attacker might be but know you will have to wait for the morning light to find out. Not wishing to spend time in the company of a corpse, you decide to sleep on the beach. Thankfully the rest of the night passes without incident, and you are relieved to see dawn finally break. You go back to the hut, where you find the body of a skinny man. Two long knives lie on the ground beside him. He has a dark moustache, a pointed beard and a thin, crooked nose. His clothing is Shazaari – loose-fitting black robes and black leggings, and a headdress made of a long black scarf wrapped around his head. His only jewellery is a silver necklace and pendant with a scorpion etching on it, which you take and put in your pocket. You also take one of the daggers from the cross belt slung around his neck. You wonder why he came to the island to kill you. Did somebody hire him to do it? If so, why? For now, there is no answer. If you want to search through the Knife Fighter's clothing, turn to **251**. If you would rather begin your daily quest for food, turn to **11**.

175

The man's aim is true, and a small dart-like arrow sinks into your leg. Lose 2 *STAMINA* points. The man sneers with satisfaction, draws a sabre from his belt and lunges at you, shouting, "I, Blackthorn of Chalice, will see your head delivered to Lord Azzur." You must fight him.

BLACKTHORN   *SKILL 8*   *STAMINA 7*

If you win, turn to **109**.

176

You open the door very slowly, mindful of traps and assassins that could be lying in wait. You hear somebody snoring and peer round the door to see a portly man with bushy eyebrows asleep in a rocking chair with his arms folded across his chest. He is wearing a white shirt tucked into a pair of baggy woollen trousers held up by bright red braces. There is a green bottle on a round wooden table next to him with a label on it which says POTION OF HEALING. Will you:

Tiptoe over to the bottle and take a swig from it? Turn to **78**
Tap the man on the shoulder to wake him up? Turn to **333**
Close the door and carry on walking east?   Turn to **277**

177

Whilst wiping the blood off your sword with some leaves, you notice an iron bracelet lying in the earth near the entrance of the den. If you want to try on the bracelet, turn to **40**. If you would rather leave it where it is and head west back to your hut on the other side of the island, turn to **217**.

178

A crowd gathers around you after your brutal battle with the Giant. You ask one of the onlookers why the Giant attacked you. He looks at you as though you are mad, and says, "What did you expect? Borg hated noise. It hurt his head and made him uncontrollably violent. That's why he lived in Quiet Street!" A murmur spreads through the crowd and suddenly a voice blurts out, "I recognize Borg's killer from the 'Wanted' posters on the noticeboards! It's the murderer! Call the Guard!" You know that nobody would believe you if you told them that you are being hunted by assassins. You must act fast. If you want to run up Quiet Street, turn to **55**. If you want to turn and run back down Quiet Street, turn to **314**.

179

The path continues to wend its way north. As you walk along, something on the ground catches your eye which is almost hidden from view by a large bush. You lift up the leaves and see a sealed wooden box. There is a message written on a label attached to the lid which reads *Property of Balthazar Wittle, The Clock Tower, Clock Street, Kaad. Do NOT open.* You shake the box and hear what sounds like metallic objects rattling around inside. If you want to break the wax seal and open the box, turn to **232**. If you would rather put the box in your backpack and carry on walking north, turn to **121**.

180

You think that the best way to put the pirates off from coming on board the *Blue Moon* is to make them believe that you have died of plague, something they would not want to catch. You uncork the bottle and quickly mark your face with red ink, highlighting your insect bites to make them look like large open sores caused by deadly smallpox. You lie down on the deck and keep perfectly still as the pirate ship comes alongside. You hear voices discussing what should be done with you. A loud gruff voice, probably that of the captain, barks out an order. "One of you dogs jump on board the boat and toss the body in the sea. Tie a rope to the boat and we'll tow it to Port Blacksand and sell it." You dare to open your eyes a fraction and see a scrawny-looking pirate standing on a plank, ready to dive into the sea. He suddenly stops in his tracks and says, "If I board that boat we're all going to die! The dead body is covered with pox! I know plague when I see it." You hear the captain order his men to set sail immediately and watch the pirate ship sail away. Moments later you see a gigantic tentacle rise out of the sea, no more than twenty metres away from the pirate ship. Another tentacle rises out of the sea, then another, and another, until there are eight tentacles towering above the ship. They belong to a giant monster from the depths of the sea which has a huge squid-like body, two massive eyes and a beaked mouth. The ship is about to be attacked by a KRAKEN. You hear booming explosions from the ship's cannon as two cannonballs whistle through the air towards the Kraken, one of them finding its mark and taking a big chunk out of one of the tentacles. The sea monster thrashes around in the sea and wraps two of its giant tentacles around the ship's mast, pulling the ship over. There is chaos on board as the Kraken slowly pulls the ship over on its side, causing everything on deck that is not lashed down to spill overboard. There is nothing the pirates can do to defeat the Kraken, and you hear them cry for help as they jump into the sea. You watch on in horror as the pirate ship disappears below the waves, and the rest of the crew with it. You trim the *Blue Moon*'s flapping sail and set a course away from the sea monster, sailing due east towards the Red River estuary. Turn to **114**.

181

You give the urchin a Gold Piece, which he bites to make sure it's real. His friends walk over, and an argument breaks out about who should keep the coin. They start pushing each other and the squabble turns into a fight.

While you are distracted by the commotion, one of the urchins deftly slips his hand inside your pocket and helps himself to your possessions. His thieving done, the pickpocket whistles to his friends, and all the urchins run off down an alleyway together, laughing loudly. You have been robbed. Lose three of the items in your pockets. You also discover the catapult is broken. Lose 1 *LUCK* point. There is little point in wasting time chasing the urchins, so you continue your walk to the Wishing Well. Turn to **261**.

182

The captain frowns and says with a grunt, "It's cold, dark and the wind is getting up. That's not good. I think we should sail to the mainland first thing tomorrow morning." If you want to insist on setting sail immediately, turn to **258**. If you want to spend one more night on the island, turn to **302**.

183

You try to dodge out of the way of the Ninja's flashing blade but suffer a deep wound on your arm. Lose 1 *SKILL* point and 4 *STAMINA* points. If you are still alive, you draw your sword to fight the quick-footed Ninja, who leaps at you, cutting his blade through the air.

NINJA WARRIOR   *SKILL* 7   *STAMINA* 6

If you win, turn to **254**.

184

You take a knife from one of the thieves and tuck it into your belt. After making sure nobody is watching, you tear down the poster, screw it into a ball and toss it away. But you know it's probably futile and that everybody in Port Blacksand is likely to be on the lookout for you, hoping to claim the reward on offer for your head. If you want to get back on board the *Blue Moon* and sail north to Red River, turn to **152**. If you want to go in the Black Lobster Tavern at the end of the quay, turn to **334**.

185

You keep your eyes on the cave, but nothing emerges from the entrance. You are about to go down the steps when you hear a rustling sound in the undergrowth behind you. You spin round to see a large humanoid creature charging straight at you with its clawed hands outstretched. Its large head is totally devoid of skin, the skull blood-red, and its protruding eyeballs and long pointed teeth hideously exposed. The repulsive beast is a seldom-seen creature of chaos known as a FLESH-HEAD. Roll two dice. If the total is equal to or less than your *SKILL* score, turn to **267**. If the number is greater than your *SKILL* score, turn to **138**.

186

The fishermen watch you carefully with their swords half-drawn as you pass by. As soon as you are far enough away they start arguing again, even louder than before. You ignore them and head north along the bank of the tributary. Turn to **47**.

187

The cupboard door is slightly ajar. You open it further with the tip of your sword and see a crimson-glazed clay pot with a cracked lid. If you want to lift the lid off the pot, turn to **122**. If you would rather not touch the pot and instead look around the cave, turn to **365**.

188

You hack at the cloud of smoke, but your sword cuts harmlessly through it and merely causes the smiling face to laugh at you silently. You grimace from the acute pain of the skeleton fingers squeezing hard on your windpipe. Lose 1 *SKILL* point and 2 *STAMINA* points. Ignoring the smoke cloud, you make a last desperate attempt to prise the remaining fingers away from your throat before you pass out. Turn to **299**.

189

You eventually come to a rickety old gate on the right which has a large sign nailed to it with the words BOGG FARM – BOG OFF painted on it. A gravel path leads from the gate to an old farmhouse, which sits in the middle of a small field separated from the grassland by a wooden fence. There is a stone post next to the gate with an arrow carved on it pointing towards the town and the words KAAD – 1 MILE underneath. From this distance, Kaad looks like it is a small town. The buildings are few in number and are mostly one or two storeys high except a stone tower in the centre of town. If you want to open the gate and walk up the path to the farmhouse, turn to **70**. If you would rather continue on to Kaad, turn to **307**.

190

You look down at the body and see your attacker is wearing the familiar silver necklace and pendant with a scorpion etching. You snap the chain and put the pendant in your pocket just as a rowdy gang of thugs rushes down on to the quayside. Several gasp in horror on seeing the man lying on the ground in a pool of blood. "Look! Lazlo

Mallick is dead!" shouts a scar-faced villain. "There's the killer!" he screams, pointing at you. "It's the same person as the one on the 'Wanted' poster!" You sweep your sword threateningly from side to side as a warning to all and tell the mob that Lazlo Mallick was an assassin who was trying to kill you. "So are we!" somebody shouts out. "A bounty of 1,000 Gold Pieces is enough to turn anybody in Port Blacksand into an assassin!" a burly rogue adds with laughter. "Let's finish this!" "After you, mate!" a skinny peg-legged pirate retorts loudly in a scratchy, high-pitched voice. Some of the villains begin chuckling, giving you a fleeting moment to cut the rope holding the *Blue Moon* to its mooring. You jump on board and cast off. "Don't let the murderer get away!" the rogue shouts angrily. The mob advances to the water's edge and starts baying for your blood. Three men dive into the water to swim after you, but with a fair wind in your sails, the *Blue Moon* quickly leaves them behind. You look back and see others jump on board a fishing boat which causes an argument, and a fight breaks out on deck. The fishing boat remains moored to the quay, and you are able to sail away on the strong easterly breeze, setting a northerly course towards the Red River estuary. You are fortunate to have escaped the mob on the wharf, but at least another assassin has been eliminated. Turn to **15**.

191

Billy smiles and says, "That seems like a very fair offer to me, brother Bobby. Throw the rope down to our new friend." You pick up the assassin's axes and climb out of the cellar and are greeted by the two Dwarfs, who slap you on the back. "No hard feelings, I hope?" says Billy. You shake your head and hand over the axes, rings and 18 Gold Pieces. The brothers shake your hand and walk with you to the wooden gate where they bid you farewell. You wave goodbye and set off towards Kaad. Turn to **307**.

192

You pull the cork out of the bottle with your teeth and hastily spread the waxy paste on the bite marks on your leg. The magic compound does its job and the wound quickly heals, leaving you feeling none the worse for the experience. You pop the small bottle inside your pocket and are about to set off again when you notice an iron bracelet lying in the earth near the entrance to the den. If you want to try on the bracelet, turn to **40**. If you would rather leave it where it is and head back to your hut on the other side of the island, turn to **217**.

193

You stand over the fallen Orc, whose death cry was heard by the main group of Orcs. More than twenty of them bear down on you, screaming and baying for your blood. Lose 1 *LUCK* point. If you have a Scroll of Invisibility, turn to **75**. If you do not have this scroll, turn to **230**.

194

A few broken planks drift past you, but nothing large enough to climb on to. You swim on until you are exhausted, at which point you can do nothing more than tread water. Suddenly you see two fins cutting through the water, moving at speed towards you. There is no mistaking the red tip of the dorsal fin of a Blood Shark. Your worst fears are about to be realized as the sharks move in for their feeding frenzy. Your adventure is over.

195

There is a full moon and everything around you looks spooky in the half-light. You find shelter under a large bush which keeps you hidden from the creatures of the night, and spend a restless night under the stars, hardly daring to go to sleep for fear of being attacked by the howling Wolves and other roaming monsters. You get up soon after dawn, feeling tired and hungry. Lose 1 *STAMINA* point. You set off immediately and pick up a trail heading north, which you decide to follow. Turn to **378**.

196

You raise your shield to ward off the flames shooting down from the sky. The flames are repelled but the shield becomes red-hot to the touch and burns the back of your arm. Lose 1 *STAMINA* point. The Dragon glides down to land on the edge of the cliff where you are standing, its gigantic clawed feet aimed directly at you. If you want to thrust your sword at the Dragon as it attempts to land, turn to **165**. If you want to run for cover, turn to **391**.

197

Mindful of the storekeeper's warning about an ambush, you slip behind a nearby tree to survey the tavern. A few minutes later you see a bald-headed man appear at an open window on the first floor holding a crossbow. He has a dent in his skull and all his teeth are made of gold. It is undoubtedly the deadly assassin Garanka Vassell. Will you:

Call out to him?	Turn to **368**
Fire an arrow at him (if you have a bow)?	Turn to **80**
Run over to the tavern door?	Turn to **42**

198

The lead shot whistles past your head and fizzes harmlessly into the sea. You hear the captain shout at his men to bring you on board his ship. If you want to cut the rope towing the *Blue Moon*, turn to **88**. If you want to give yourself up to the pirates, turn to **290**.

199

After handing over your possessions, you are led below decks to the galley, where you are ordered to help the ship's cook prepare the iron rations for the crew. Your first job is to pick maggots out of the dried meat and scrape the weevils off the sea biscuits. The smell of rotten food in the galley makes you feel sick, but you know it won't be too long before the ship reaches Port Blacksand. You keep your head down and only speak when spoken to as the old ship creaks and shudders its way across the open sea. Your disgusting job is almost completed when you suddenly hear shouting coming from the upper deck, and the captain screaming out orders to his helmsman to turn the ship hard to starboard. You run over to look through a porthole on the port side and are alarmed to see a gigantic tentacle rising out of the sea, no more than twenty metres away from the ship. Another tentacle rises out of the sea, then another, and another, until there are eight of them towering above you. The ship is about to be attacked by a KRAKEN, a giant sea monster with a colossal squid-like body, two huge eyes and a beaked mouth. You hear booming explosions from the ship's cannon as two cannonballs whistle through the air towards the Kraken, one of them finding its mark and taking a big chunk out of one of the tentacles. The sea monster retaliates by wrapping two of its giant tentacles around the ship's mast. There is chaos on board as the Kraken starts pulling the ship over on to its side. You hear the pirates cry for help as they jump into the sea, and it's all you can do to hang on as water bursts into the ship's galley. The cook scrambles up the stairs and disappears, leaving you all alone. You grab his meat cleaver and follow him up on deck as the ship starts to sink. You see some pirates trying their best to launch a rowing boat, but the ship is heeled over, which makes their task impossibly difficult. If you want to help them launch the rowing boat, turn to **85**. If you would rather make your way to the back of the ship, cut the rope towing the *Blue Moon*, and jump into the sea to climb on board, turn to **304**.

200

The sweeping plain is grassland as far as you can see all the way to the town in the far distance. The path cuts a straight line through the tall grasses and you follow it north for a while before turning right to follow the path heading north-east. You walk along it for some time until you arrive at a junction with another narrow path. If you want to head west along the new path, turn to **135**. If you want to keep going north-east towards the town, turn to **369**.

201

You peer inside the gloomy cave and see a coil of rope

hanging on a rusty iron peg just inside the entrance. You look up and see hundreds of black bats hanging upside down from the ceiling. There isn't much light, just enough to see what looks like a small wooden cupboard mounted on the wall at the back of the cave. If you want to take the rope, turn to **331**. If you would rather walk over to the cupboard at the back of the cave, turn to **187**.

202

The little man scrambles down the tree and introduces himself. "Hello, my name is Gerrit. I'm a Woodling. We live in the trees because there are just too many terrifying monsters stalking the forest. Some we can hide from, some we can run from, some we can slay, but none of us has ever defeated a Shape Changer or escaped from the jaws of a Giant Slugworm. What's your story?" You hand Gerrit two rations from your Provisions (deduct these from your *Adventure Sheet*) and tell him about Lord Azzur and the assassination attempts on your life. He looks at you aghast and says, "Don't chance going in the forest. You should go to Kaad immediately. A passing trapper told me that Azzur was in town! Walk east around the edge of the forest and you'll eventually see Kaad. You can't miss it." If you want to take Gerrit's advice and head east, turn to **328**. If you would rather ignore his advice and go in the forest, turn to **51**.

He is fast asleep and snoring loudly

203

You set off at a brisk pace, following a well-worn path along the riverbank. Up ahead you see a small man lying on the ground, his back propped up against a tree and his arms folded across his chest. He's wearing a dark green tunic and brown leggings which are tucked into his green leather boots. A floppy green felt hat is pulled down low over his face. He is fast asleep and snoring loudly. If you want to wake him up to speak to him, turn to **68**. If you would rather keep heading east, turn to **244**.

204

You climb up the tree as fast as you can and stand still on a high branch. You suddenly notice a large bird's nest in the fork of the branch above in which two Death Hawk chicks start screeching loudly. *Test Your Luck*. If you are Lucky, turn to **41**. If you are Unlucky, turn to **115**.

205

You do not have to wait long before somebody responds to your call for help. You sense somebody is standing behind you, watching, and your worst fears are confirmed when you realize it is not the trapper. "Thank you for calling out to me! I'm surprised my fellow assassins failed to slay you when you make it so easy to find you. Lord Azzur will be pleased with the gift I will bring him in the morning and I will be 10,000 Gold Pieces the richer." Caught in the trap, there is nothing you can do to defend yourself from the strike of the assassin's blade. Your adventure is over.

206

You are caught by the fiery blast which burns your flesh badly. Lose 1 *SKILL* point and 4 *STAMINA* points. The pain is terrible, but there is no time to think about it as the Dragon glides down to land on the edge of the cliff where you are standing with its gigantic clawed feet aimed directly at you. If you want to thrust your sword at the Dragon as it attempts to land, turn to **165**. If you want to run for cover, turn to **391**.

207

Much to your relief, the bystanders do not pay you any attention. Your brief time in Kaad has been a battle for survival and, not wishing to get into any bloodier battles, you decide to head for the main gates and leave town. You walk down Clock Street, which takes you to the market square and on down Crown Street to the main gates. There aren't many people about other than a few merchants leaving town after a long day at the market. As you walk out through the gates, a mean-looking man in a hooded black cloak and a bow and quiver of arrows slung over his shoulder rides past you on a black horse. He glances down at you as he passes by and spits on the ground. If you want to ask him for a ride, turn to **303**. If you want to carry on walking, turn to **252**.

208

Sidd leans forward and slowly opens the wooden box. He reaches inside and lifts out a clear glass ball which has multicoloured gases swirling around inside it. Holding it aloft on the fingertips of one hand, he closes his eyes and begins talking in a language you do not understand. The swirling gases suddenly clear, and inside the crystal ball you see a horse-drawn carriage speeding along a dusty road. The Seer opens his eyes again and the image disappears. "Azzur left Port Blacksand early this morning and will soon be arriving in Kaad. You should head north if you hope to catch him. I'm risking my life telling you the whereabouts of the Dark Lord so a payment of 1 Gold Piece would seem fair, don't you think?" Sidd says, holding out his hand. If you want to pay him, turn to **282**. If you want to leave without paying, turn to **372**.

209

There is nobody looking out to sea from the stern of the pirate ship, and you slip unseen on board the *Blue Moon*. It's a bumpy ride, but you make great headway being towed along by the pirate ship. If you want to continue being towed to Port Blacksand, turn to **5**. If you want to cut the rope that is towing the *Blue Moon*, turn to **88**.

210

You instinctively reach up and grab hold of a large black spider with its long hairy legs wriggling in your hand. You feel a sharp pain in one of your fingers. You have been bitten by a poisonous spider. Lose 2 *STAMINA* points. You throw it on to the ground and crush it underfoot. You suck out the poison, spit it out, then walk on towards Kaad, crossing a field to a dirt road which leads to the main entrance gates of town. You see a horse-drawn open carriage coming out through the gates driven by a man wearing a bowler hat and a tailored waistcoat over his crisp white shirt. Sitting bolt upright next to him, looking snootily down her nose with an air of grand superiority, is a rosy-cheeked woman wearing a floral hat and long baggy black dress. If you want to put your hand up to stop the carriage to talk to the woman, turn to **120**. If you want to keep your head down and enter Kaad, turn to **390**.

211

The Monk drops his sack on the ground, and says:

> "The sack is certainly very full
> But it's mostly balls of orange wool
> A woolly jumper I will knit
> To keep me warm through the wintry bit
> The only thing I have to sell
> Is a map leading to the Wishing Well."

He stares at you fiercely with one eyebrow raised and demands 5 Gold Pieces for his map. If you have 5 Gold Pieces and wish to buy the map, turn to **117**. If you do not have 5 Gold Pieces or do not want to buy the map, turn to **3**.

212

Luckily, the barrel does not topple over. You kick out again, harder this time, which forces the Rat to loosen its grip on your boot. You regain your balance and jump up to grab the top of the wall, pulling yourself up just as the crowd is closing in. You look down and see the Armed Guards arguing about who should be giving who a leg up to climb over the wall. You leave them to it and jump down into the back yard of a small house. There is a pile of coal in one corner of the yard and you can feel the heat from the fire of an open furnace nearby. There is an anvil next to the furnace and a hammer and tongs hanging from hooks on the wall. You notice the back door of the house is ajar and there is a passageway running down the side of the house to the street. If you want to go into the house, turn to **98**. If you want to walk down the side passage, turn to **330**.

213

You reach the east side of the island in less than an hour, emerging from the undergrowth on to a rocky open area which ends at the edge of a cliff. There is a beach below and you notice a cave entrance at the base of the cliff. There are some rough stone steps leading down to the beach. If you want to walk down the steps and enter the cave, turn to **294**. If you would rather wait to see if there is any sign of life inside the cave, turn to **185**.

214

Fighting for your life, you just manage to gather enough strength to prise one of the fingers away from your throat. You snap it off and a wisp of green smoke escapes from the hollow of the broken finger, forming a small cloud in the shape of a grinning face of an evil spirit. If you want to continue trying to prise the other fingers away from your throat, turn to **299**. If you want to take a swipe at the smoke cloud, turn to **188**.

215

The storekeeper looks at you in disbelief, and says abruptly, "As you wish. I'm going home now. You're on your own. Good luck." The storekeeper begins closing the window shutters and asks you to leave whilst he locks up. You have no option but to leave the store and head east on foot. Turn to **203**.

216

Azzur looks at you closely, nodding his head several times deep in thought. "That's an impressive number," he says coldly. Turn to **276**.

217

You hack your way through the undergrowth, being careful not to brush against the poison-tipped creepers. You hear the sound of buzzing overhead and look up to see a swarm of bees fly out of their hive high up in a tree. If you want to climb the tree to see if you can find some honey, turn to **370**. If you would rather press on to get back to your hut, turn to **147**.

218

The Luck Gods smile on you and decide that yours is a Ring of Good Fortune. Add 1 *SKILL* point, 2 *STAMINA* points and 3 *LUCK* points. You put the clock hands back in the box and place it back under the bush before setting off north again in good spirits. Turn to **121**.

219

You attack the rats, hacking at them furiously with your sword. You are bitten several times by some which run up your leg. Lose 2 *STAMINA* points. More rats swarm out of the drain and you soon realize there are just too many of them for you to overcome. You give up trying and walk back up the stairs to where Balthazar is waiting. "Call yourself a rat catcher? If you think I'm going to pay you, you can think again! You can go now. I'm going to get somebody else to do the job." He opens the front door and signals for you to leave. You barge past him and turn right up Clock Street. Turn to **89**.

220

The intruder's dagger strikes you, but only causes a light flesh wound to your arm. Lose 2 *STAMINA* points. You retaliate by swiping your sword through the darkness, and feel it strike home. A man's muffled cry breaks the silence, and you hear him stumble backwards. You step forward to finish off the intruder, who is a skilful KNIFE FIGHTER. Although injured, he is agile and quick on his feet, and you must fight him in total darkness.

KNIFE FIGHTER   *SKILL 7*   *STAMINA 6*

If you win, turn to **174**.

221

The apple is crisp and tasty, and just what you need after a long walk. You help yourself to a second apple and devour it just as quickly as the first one. Add 2 *STAMINA* points. You look round but there is nobody to thank, so you set off east again. Turn to **358**.

An unpleasant smell suddenly fills your nostrils

222

You walk east some distance until you come to a junction in the path where it meets another path running north-south. You don't see any point in going back south so you turn left to head north towards the town, which you can see in the distance. Turn to **369**.

223

You set off again, picking a path through the thick undergrowth, wondering what other strange things you might discover on the creepy island. It's not long before you find out. An unpleasant smell suddenly fills your nostrils – a foul stench like rotten eggs. There is a strange mound in front of you, something that resembles a huge lump of green wax. Suddenly it moves, rising up slowly on its trunklike legs. It is a huge creature with an enormous oval head and tiny sunken eyes, two small holes for a nose, and a gaping fanged mouth from which drool dribbles down its multilayered chin. It is covered with open sores which ooze thick, yellow pus which trickles down its bloated body like melting candle wax. A swarm of flies buzzes around the creature, landing on it to feed on its stinking excretions. The creature's noxious smell makes you light-headed and you start to feel dizzy. If you want to stand your ground and fight the DECAYER, turn to **306**. If you would rather flee, turn to **359**.

224

You enter a musty-smelling candlelit room which has an enormous bookcase set against the far wall. The shelves are crammed full of ancient leather-bound tomes. There is a table and chair in the middle of the room, with several books lying open on the table. The woman invites you to look at a book entitled *Dragonfire*. As you flick through the pages you see her glance over your shoulder. Her smile vanishes, and the door suddenly slams shut behind you. You spin round to see the man who was hiding behind it. Dressed head to toe in loose black robes, all you can see of his face are his stone-cold brown eyes. Holding his straight-bladed short sword above his head in both hands is a NINJA WARRIOR who utters a shrill battle cry and leaps forward to attack you. If your current *SKILL* score is 8 or greater, turn to **93**. If your *SKILL* is 7 or less, turn to **183**.

225

You feel a sharp pain as one of the daggers finds its mark, hitting you squarely in the shoulder. Lose 2 *STAMINA* points. Not stopping to look back at the angry mob, you run through the tavern doorway and on down to the quayside. Turn to **234**.

226

You notice that some of the people standing at the crossroads are armed with clubs and pitchforks, and you suspect they are probably looking for you. You pretend to scratch your head as you walk past them, trying to hide your face. *Test Your Luck*. If you are Lucky, turn to **207**. If you are Unlucky, turn to **284**.

227

You look at the bite marks on your leg and are horrified to see tiny white thread-like worms wriggling around in the wound. You scrape them off with your knife, but there is nothing you can do to rid yourself of the virus the worms have infected you with. You break out in a sweat and suddenly feel very unwell. You get hotter and hotter as the virus takes hold and you soon pass out. Only people with a strong constitution can survive the Gungh Virus. Lose 10 *STAMINA* points. If you are still alive, turn to **398**.

228

You catch sight of a small deer grazing in the warm sunshine. You walk towards it but as soon as it sees you it bounds off and disappears into the long grass. You walk back to the path, and step on something metallic which was hidden from view by the grass. *Test Your Luck*. If you are Lucky, turn to **332**. If you are Unlucky, turn to **148**.

229

The storekeeper frowns, and says solemnly, "Yes, I've heard of him. He paid me an unwelcome visit earlier today. He barged in, spat on the floor and made a horrible smell. Then he helped himself to my food, took an axe, some rope and didn't pay me a penny. A disgusting human being if ever there was one. He put up the 'Wanted' poster on the wall outside, which, as you know, has your face displayed on it. When he finally spoke, he told me his name and said that if I saw you, I was to tell you I had seen him in Tall Tom's Tavern, which is half an hour's walk east of here. Then I was supposed to light a fire and cover it with wet leaves to make a smoke signal to let him know you were on your way, so he could ambush you. Don't worry, that's not going to happen. Harold Cornpepper is not in the habit of helping assassins. If you are the valiant warrior who defeated Zanbar Bone, Allansia will be forever in your debt. However, Lord Azzur will not rest until you are dead. You will need to be prepared for when you meet Vassell. Might I suggest you purchase one or two magic items from my display case?" You thank the storekeeper for his advice and decide what to do. If you want to look at the items in the display case, turn to **54**. If you want to leave the store straight away and head east in pursuit of Garanka Vassell, turn to **203**.

230

The band of screaming Orcs crashes into you with the force of a herd of stampeding Hippohogs. Their flailing swords, axes, morning stars and cudgels make light work of your pitiful resistance, and the battle lasts less than a minute. Your adventure is over.

231

A search of the beach yields a silver coin buried in the sand and a rusty old knife which you find in a rock pool. You put the items in your pocket and look out to sea to spot a barrel bobbing up and down which appears to be attached to the seabed by a rope or a chain. If you want to swim out to the barrel, turn to **255**. If you would rather climb back up the stone steps to the top of the cliff, turn to **127**.

232

You hear a faint click when you lift the lid. A small dart shoots out of the box and lodges painfully in your shoulder. Lose 2 *STAMINA* points. Inside the box you find 10 Gold Pieces, two long brass clock hands and a gold signet ring with a question mark engraved on it. You pocket the Gold Pieces and examine the ring. If you want to try it on, turn to **346**. If you would rather put the ring and the clock hands back in the box and place it back under the bush and continue north, turn to **121**.

233

One by one, the contestants are introduced to Baron Sukumvit and Lord Azzur. When your turn comes, the Baron asks you to remove your helmet before stepping on to the podium out of respect for his guest. If you want to take off your helmet, turn to **145**. If you want to refuse to take it off for fear of being recognized, turn to **366**.

234

Port Blacksand is not the place where you want to be right now, and you run as fast as you can down the quay to where the *Blue Moon* is moored. Leaning against the bollard is an unshaven, one-armed beggar with his head bowed. His dirty, baggy shirt and ragged cotton pants are partially covered by a moth-eaten blanket. He rattles his tin mug at you and says in a quivering voice, "Spare me a coin and I'll untie your boat for you." If you want to give the beggar a coin to help you cast off, turn to **389**. If you want to ignore him and untie the mooring rope yourself before jumping on board your boat, turn to **129**.

235

You scramble down the tree and land on top of the Orc who is waiting below. He is armed with a morning star and you strike him a mighty blow with your sword before he can stand up. Blood pours from the Orc's side, and although badly injured, he manages to get back up on his feet. The Orc staggers towards you, spitting blood and roaring in pain, swinging his morning star. You must finish off the Orc quickly before the other Orcs hear the commotion.

ORC   *SKILL 6*   *STAMINA 2*

If you win the fight in the first Attack Round, turn to **311**. If it takes two or more Attack Rounds to defeat the Orc, turn to **193**.

236

You swerve sharply left and keep on running, just in time, as flames shoot down and scorch the ground where you were a second ago. With its giant leathery wings flapping noisily above you, the Dragon climbs into the sky, ready to swoop down to attack you again with its fiery breath. Running into the undergrowth, you spot the entrance to a burrow in the ground, perhaps a den made by a wild animal. If you want to jump down feet first into the burrow to hide from the Dragon, turn to **285**. If you want to keep on running, turn to **325**.

237

The tip of the dart is coated in toxic snake venom and you immediately start to shake uncontrollably. Lose 10 *STAMINA* points. If you are still alive, turn to **271**.

238

The arrow flies straight and true through the open window, and you hear a scream of pain. Your arrow has struck its target, and you punch the air in triumph. Gain 1 *LUCK* point. But your joy is short-lived because suddenly the tavern door bursts open. A heavily built man storms out of the tavern, screaming at the top of his voice, and charges at you like a raging bull, swinging a two-handed sword above his head. There is an arrow shaft sticking out of the fleshy part of his neck, but it doesn't appear to bother Garanka Vassell. You draw your sword and ready yourself to fight the deadly assassin. Turn to **53**.

239

The pirates are astonished to see you kill their captain. They are very angry and start yelling at you and close in with their cutlasses drawn. Will you:

Stand your ground and fight them?	Turn to **340**
Climb the rigging and tell the motley crew that you have appointed yourself as their new captain?	Turn to **79**
Jump over the side and swim to the *Blue Moon*?	Turn to **24**

240

Brother Billy scratches his head and says, "Well, that sounds like a load of hogwash to me. What do you think, brother Bobby?" Bobby scratches his head and says, "I think you are probably right, brother Billy. Maybe it's time we let the trespasser play our favourite game!" "Great idea, brother Bobby," says Billy. Turn to **381**.

241

You come to the foot of a small hill and run up and over it and down to a wooded area, where you see a silver-haired woman standing in a doorway which has been cut out of the trunk of a huge oak tree. "Over here!" she cries, beckoning you over to her. "Quick, come inside and close the door behind you!" If you want to follow her through the doorway, turn to **63**. If you would rather keep on running, turn to **316**.

242

You pass by a dead tree devoid of bark and leaves where a skeleton hand is hanging on a rusty nail hammered into the trunk. The bones are well weathered, dark ochre in colour, and look to have been hanging on the nail for years. If you want to lift the dismembered hand off the nail, turn to **343**. If you would rather leave it where it is and walk on, turn to **223**.

She is whistling happily to herself

243

You walk through the main gates and mingle with the townsfolk, who are busily going about their various tasks. Nobody pays you much attention as you walk down Crown Street, which is lined on both sides with small shops and old wood and plaster houses with tiled roofs. The street leads into the market square, where the traders are packing up their stalls for the day. You see a portly man in long brown robes walking towards you carrying a large sack over his shoulder. If you want to talk to him, turn to **19**. If you would rather ignore him and walk across the market square to Clock Street, turn to **140**.

244

Looking south, you see a ruined tower some distance away on the other side of the river. As though spooked by your gaze, a large flock of crows takes flight from the ruins, cawing loudly. You walk on, and it's not long before you see a woman in a cloak with the hood down walking towards you along the path. She is whistling happily to herself whilst sharpening one end of a stick with a knife and doesn't seem bothered when she sees you. She has a quiver of arrows slung over her shoulders but is not carrying a bow. When she is close, she stops and says with a beaming smile, "Greetings!" If you want to talk to her, turn to **362**. If you would rather bid her good day and carry on walking east, turn to **298**.

245

You feel a sharp pain in your side as the lead shot from the captain's pistol grazes your flesh. Lose 2 *STAMINA* points. You hear the captain singing his own praises loudly about his shooting skills. He orders his men to bring you on board his ship and disappears out of sight. If you want to cut the rope towing the *Blue Moon*, turn to **88**. If you want to give yourself up to the pirates, turn to **290**.

246

The chain mail vest is heavy but will protect you in battle. Add 1 *SKILL* point. Pleased with your new armour, you think about what to do next. Will you:

Go in the tavern?	Turn to **341**
Head north along a new path?	Turn to **133**
Continue your journey east?	Turn to **157**

247

The relentless blows from the Berserker's battleaxe are impossible to withstand. He swings his axe with superhuman strength, and it is all you can do to parry the giant blade. You are forced backwards and stumble over a tree root. He grunts with satisfaction and strikes again, and you suffer a deep wound to your thigh. Lose 2 *STAMINA* points. If you are still alive, turn to **106**.

248

You manage to navigate the rough stone steps without falling and run as fast as you can across the sandy beach, diving into the sea with the swarm of bees trailing behind you. You stay underwater as long as you can, and it's only when your lungs feel as though they are about to burst that you surface to breathe in the fresh air. Much to your relief, the bees have flown off. Unfortunately, half of your remaining Provisions are nothing but a soggy mess at the bottom of your backpack. Delete them from your *Adventure Sheet*. After drying yourself off, you climb back up the steps and head west back to your hut on the other side of the island. Turn to **147**.

249

You hear footsteps approaching, and see the door opened by a bespectacled, jovial-looking man with thinning grey hair and long bushy sideburns almost down to his chin. He's wearing a waistcoat over a baggy white shirt tucked into his checked trousers, which are held up by red braces. He peers over the top of his spectacles and says, "Hello, I'm Balthazar Wittle. Are you the rat catcher?" If you want to reply "Yes", turn to **383**. If you want to reply "No", turn to **30**.

250

You hand over 2 Gold Pieces in payment for six arrows, which you notice all have flights made with black feathers. The fletcher sees you looking at them and says, "The flights are made from chicken feathers, which ensures my arrows fly true. Is there anything else you would like to know?" If you want to ask her if she has heard any rumours about assassins in the area, turn to **164**. If you would rather set off east again, turn to **279**.

251

You find a small circular brass box with a hinged lid concealed in a hidden pocket inside the Knife Fighter's robes. There is a silver ring inside the box. If you want to try on the ring, turn to **322**. If you would rather begin your quest for food for the third day, turn to **11**.

252

You set off at a brisk pace in the direction of Fang, hoping to find shelter before the sun disappears below the horizon. The light gradually fades, and shadows begin to creep over the Pagan Plain. Howls and growls from the creatures of the night break the silence as they ready themselves for their nightly hunt. All you see is scrubland for miles around and, unable to find a shelter, you are forced to sleep under a large bush, which at least hides you from prying eyes. There is a full moon and everything around you looks spooky in the half-light. You spend a restless night under the stars, hardly daring to go to sleep for fear of being attacked by Wolves or other flesh-eating creatures you hear roaming about. You get up soon after dawn, feeling tired and hungry. Lose 1 *STAMINA* point. You set off again, passing a log cabin in the west, and pick up a trail heading north, which you decide to follow. Turn to **378**.

253

You watch the barman shrug his shoulders and nonchalantly tap a bottle with a spoon several times and call for silence in the tavern. "Look who we've got here!" he shouts out to his customers while pointing at you. Everybody in the tavern turns towards you. Several unsavoury-looking villains stand up, daggers in hand. "It's the murderer!" shouts one of the crooks. "It's more like 1,000 Gold Pieces on legs!" cries an old pickpocket with glee. Surrounded by the noisy mob, you decide to run for it. You kick over the table in front of you and dash for the door. Although the crowd is distracted by the flying table, three thieves manage to throw their daggers at you. *Test Your Luck.* If you are Lucky, turn to **73**. If you are Unlucky, turn to **225**.

254

When you reach down to uncover the Ninja's face, the woman flees from the room and runs up the stairs. You hear the door open and close but let her go, as you are more interested to see if the Ninja was another of Lord Azzur's assassins. The silver pendant hanging on the chain around his neck answers your question. You snap the chain and pocket the silver scorpion. You find the name Gozo Yamakuri embroidered on his robes and see that he was also wearing a thin copper headband. You empty the Ninja's cloth backpack and find a pair of bone dice and some rice wrapped in broad leaves. You eat the rice, which eases your hunger and gives you some energy. Add 2 *STAMINA* points. Will you:

Try on the headband?	Turn to **118**
Look at the books on the bookshelves?	Turn to **355**
Walk up the stairs and go back outside?	Turn to **305**

255

You leave your possessions on the beach and swim out to sea with your knife gripped between your teeth. The water is cold but the current isn't very strong, and you are able to swim towards the barrel without much effort. You are about fifteen metres away from it when you see something moving towards you on the surface of the water. The huge fanged jaw of a sea creature suddenly opens up in front of you. It is a GIANT SEA SNAKE, some ten metres long, and you must fight it with your knife. Reduce your *SKILL* by 2 points for this battle.

GIANT SEA SNAKE   *SKILL* 7   *STAMINA* 7

If you win, turn to **104**.

256

You instinctively reach up and grab hold of the large yellow spider with its long hairy legs wriggling in your hand. Luckily it isn't poisonous. You toss it into the long grass and walk on towards Kaad, crossing a field to a dirt road which leads to the main entrance gates of town. You see a horse-drawn open carriage coming out through the gates driven by a man wearing a bowler hat and a tailored waistcoat over his crisp white shirt. Sitting bolt upright next to him, looking snootily down her nose with an air of grand superiority, is a rosy-cheeked woman wearing a floral hat and long baggy black dress. If you want to put your hand up to stop the carriage and talk to the woman, turn to **120**. If you want to keep your head down and enter Kaad, turn to **390**.

257

Sidd leans forward and slowly opens the wooden box. He reaches inside and lifts out a glass ball which has colourful gases swirling around inside it. Holding it aloft on the fingertips of one hand, he closes his eyes and begins talking in a language you do not understand. The swirling gases suddenly clear, and inside the crystal ball you see a tall warrior woman armed with a spear running along a dirt path at speed. She has striking silver markings covering much of her bronzed skin and her hair is close-cropped and dyed scarlet red. The Seer opens his eyes again and the image vanishes and says, "Ren-Ren Pakk is on her way to hunt you down. She is a Zengian Ultra, a fanatical fighter who is fleet of foot and has lightning reflexes. She will be a formidable opponent." You thank Sidd for the information and wish him farewell. Tall Tom says goodbye, telling you to come back one day. You walk out of the tavern and think about which way to go. If you want to head north, turn to **133**. If you want to continue east, turn to **157**.

258

You tell him that there is no time to lose, and that you have to find Garanka Vassell or whichever assassin is coming for you next before they find you. You jump on board whilst the captain unfurls the sails and casts off into choppy waters. You peer out to sea, wondering if you will be able to defeat Azzur's assassins. The wind soon starts to howl under the darkening skies, with the boat bobbing up and down on the rough sea and the rigging creaking under the strain. Rain lashes down, and the old boat is battered by high waves crashing over the deck, forcing you to hang on to the rigging to stop yourself from being washed overboard into the churning sea. "We should turn back," the captain shouts into your ear. But before you have time to reply, a bolt of lightning shoots down from the dark sky. *Test Your Luck.* If you are Lucky, turn to **373**. If you are Unlucky, turn to **154**.

259

Azzur rubs his hands together, enjoying the moment. The Guards become restless and inch forward, desperate to be told to drag you away in chains. The Baron raises his hand and the Guards immediately stand upright, rigid as statues. Azzur walks slowly to the front of the podium and looks you in the eye. "Now tell me, cockroach, how many pendants do you have exactly?" he asks with a snarl. Will you reply:

Seven	Turn to **49**
Nine	Turn to **92**
Eleven	Turn to **171**
Thirteen	Turn to **216**
Fifteen	Turn to **357**

260

As you draw your sword, the Monk sighs, shakes his head, and thrusts out his right hand towards you. A zigzag bolt of lightning shoots out from his hand and slams into your chest, knocking you off your feet and making you lose consciousness. Lose 1 *SKILL* point and 5 *STAMINA* points. If you are still alive, turn to **354**.

261

You follow the map past a junction with Brick Street into Quiet Street where, strangely, all the people are tiptoeing along in bare feet with their shoes tucked under their arms. Everybody is communicating by gesture and nobody is making a sound. An old woman wearing a headscarf looks fiercely at you and puts her index finger to her lips and points at your boots. If you want to take off your boots, turn to **335**. If you want to keep them on, turn to **360**.

262

You swing your sword through the air, but the Dragon pulls its feet up just in time, and you fail to hit your target. Before you have time to strike again, the Dragon lashes out once more with its clawed feet, grabbing you by your head and squeezing it hard. You immediately lose consciousness. The Dragon has caught its prey and it won't go hungry today. Your adventure is over.

263

You walk quietly away from the Orcs, who you can hear shouting and arguing behind you in the clearing. You make your way north through the wood and over a small hill down to a huge grass-covered plain. You see two paths in front of you. One path heads due north towards a forest and the other leads off it and heads north-east towards a town in the far distance. If you want to take the path heading north towards the forest, turn to **101**. If you want to follow this path as far as the junction and take the new path towards the town, turn to **200**.

264

You open the creaking door and enter a large candlelit room which has a large collection of monster-head trophies mounted on the walls. A red-haired man with rosy cheeks and curly sideburns is sitting behind the wooden counter reading a book with thick, wire-rimmed round spectacles perched halfway down his nose. There is a blunderbuss on the shelf on the wall behind the man. "Good evening. Welcome to Otto's Outpost. I hope you had a pleasant journey here?" the man says jovially, peering over the top of his spectacles. "I presume you are wanting a room for the night? That will cost you the princely sum of 1 Gold Piece, including breakfast. Does that meet with your approval?" If you want to pay 1 Gold Piece to stay at Otto's Outpost, turn to **339**. If you would rather go back outside and spend the night under the stars on the open plain, turn to **195**.

265

You just manage to swim over to the *Blue Moon* before the Blood Sharks arrive. You grab hold of the side of the boat and haul yourself on board, panting hard. You know your only chance of survival is to act quickly and cut the rope attached to the grappling hook. Turn to **88**.

266

The warrior bears down on you and at the last moment leaps in the air and lands on you, wielding her long knives around furiously. She strikes you before you even know it. Lose 2 *STAMINA* points. You stagger back and watch the wild-eyed warrior stand still for a second with her head tilted to one side before uttering her shrill war cry and attacking you again in a flurry of flashing blades.

ZENGIAN ULTRA　　　　　*SKILL 9*　　*STAMINA 6*

If you win, turn to **22**.

267

You just manage to sidestep out of the path of the oncoming Flesh-Head, which flies at full speed over the edge of the cliff. It lands head first on the jagged rocks below and is killed instantly. You walk rapidly down the stone steps to the beach below, where you find a large ruby set in the navel of the Flesh-Head. Add 1 *LUCK* point. You prise it out without any fuss and pocket the gem before walking over to the mouth of the cave. Turn to **201**.

"I think my wish has just come true!"

268

You enter the hedge-lined gardens and walk along a gravel path to a white marble fountain where water is pouring from four serpent-headed spouts into a large pool which contains hundreds of coins. There is a short, stocky man with long hair, tanned skin and narrow eyes standing on the other side of the fountain. He is wearing a red silk neckerchief and sleeveless leather jerkin over his collarless shirt. His sleeves are rolled up and you see his arms are completely covered in snake tattoos. He is holding a black stick in one hand and casually tosses a coin into the fountain with his free hand. He watches the coin sink to the bottom and then turns to you, smiles and says, "I think my wish has just come true!" He suddenly puts the stick to his lips and exhales sharply. A small dart shoots out and hits you in the neck. His stick is a blowpipe. If you are wearing a Snakefang earring, turn to **141**. If you are not wearing the earring, turn to **237**.

269

A crossbow bolt slams into your lower back with a sickening thud. Lose 1 *SKILL* point and 4 *STAMINA* points. The pain in your back is excruciating when you pull the bolt out, but there is no time to treat the wound as the tavern door bursts open. A bald-headed man wearing a chain mail vest storms out of the tavern screaming, and charges at you like a raging bull, swinging a two-handed sword above his head. You notice that he has a dent in his skull and all his teeth are made of gold. It is the deadly assassin Garanka Vassell and you must fight him. Turn to **53**.

270

A large wooden barrel drifts past you which looks to be just about big enough for you to climb into. You swim over to it and lift the lid to discover that it is half full of bananas. You climb inside the barrel, and are just able to stand up, waist-high in bananas. You eat your fill, thinking how fortunate you are to be alive. Add 1 *LUCK* point and 1 *STAMINA* point. You haul a small plank out of the water which you use as a crude paddle to steer yourself east towards the mainland. Apart from some Blood Sharks circling you at one point, the voyage to the mainland passes without incident. A strong easterly wind helps speed up the journey in your makeshift craft, and several hours later the rugged Allansian coastline comes into view. The cliffs are quite high, but you see an estuary directly ahead which you know to be the entrance to Red River. An hour later and you are at the mouth of the river, where you see two wooden buildings on the northern bank. You steer the barrel over to the bank and climb out. It feels great to be back on dry land, but you are also very aware that Lord Azzur has his best assassins hunting you down to relieve you of your head. If only Captain Crow had told you who the other assassins were before he died, you would be better prepared. Now everybody you meet could be an assassin. But at least you should recognize Garanka Vassell when you see him, if not the other assassins. You walk towards the buildings, which you see are a boatyard and a general store. You have no reason to visit the boatyard and walk past it. If you want to go in the general store, turn to **327**. If you would rather head east, turn to **203**.

271

The partial paralysis is short-lived and you somehow manage to clear your head. You draw your sword and stagger forward to fight Tunku Yang, the notorious Poisoner of Kay-Pong. He curses, annoyed that you have survived his poisoned dart, and lunges at you armed with only a dagger.

TUNKU YANG   *SKILL 5*   *STAMINA 6*

If you lose an *Attack Round*, turn to **59**. If you win without losing an *Attack Round*, turn to **326**.

272

Running down the steps, you lose your footing and fall off the path, tumbling head over heels on to the beach below. You land on a patch of soft sand but still sprain your neck badly. Lose 1 *SKILL* point and 1 *STAMINA* point. You pick yourself up and run as fast as you can across the beach, diving into the sea with the swarm of bees trailing behind you. You stay underwater as long as you can, and it's only when your lungs feel as though they are about to burst that you surface to breathe in fresh air. Much to your relief, the bees have flown off. Unfortunately, half of your remaining Provisions are nothing but a soggy mess at the bottom of your backpack. Delete them from your *Adventure Sheet*. After drying yourself off, you climb back up the steps and head west back to your hut on the other side of the island. Turn to **147**.

273

The Luck Gods are unhappy and decide that yours is a Ring of Ill Fortune. Lose 1 *SKILL* point, 2 *STAMINA* points and 3 *LUCK* points. You put the clock hands back in the box and place it back under the bush before setting off north again, annoyed with yourself for having tempted fate. Turn to **121**.

274

The woman shuts the door quickly behind her just as the Orcs appear on the top of the hill. The bark-covered door fits the doorway so tightly that nobody would know it was there. You run on with the Orcs charging down the hill after you in hot pursuit. They pursue you relentlessly, and when they are just a few metres behind, you have no choice but to turn and face them. Turn to **230**.

275

As you turn to head back, a thick vine wraps itself around your ankle, and another creeps out from under the dense foliage to wrap around your other leg. You try hacking at the vines with your sword, but more vines slide out and ensnare your arms. The vines tighten, and you are unable to move as a long tendril uncoils from the second Bloodwort hidden in the undergrowth and hovers in front of your face. You scream in terror as it inches towards your mouth and plunges down your throat. The fibrous tendril is too tough to bite through, and you start to choke. You feel a violent pain as the tendril begins to drain your stomach and suck the life from your body. You see Captain Crow's eyes are shut, his struggles over, and it won't be long before yours are too. Your adventure is over.

276

"Congratulations," Lord Azzur says begrudgingly. "I thought it would be impossible to defeat all my assassins. You are truly a champion warrior. If circumstances were different we might have been able to work together. I thought that would be impossible since you killed my master, Zanbar Bone. But on reflection, maybe it was meant to be. Maybe I will rule Allansia one day without needing the help of the Demon Prince. And maybe you deserve the chance of freedom. Your fighting skills have certainly earned you the right to represent me in the Trial of Champions. So that's what you will do. Should you survive, the 10,000 Gold Piece prize will be mine, of course, but I will grant you a full pardon for your crimes and give you your freedom." Inside you are raging with anger but realize that attempting to slay Azzur now would inevitably result in certain death. If you want to accept your fate and enter Deathrap Dungeon, turn to **347**. If you want to refuse to enter Deathtrap Dungeon, turn to **366**.

277

Half an hour later you arrive at a tributary which joins the Red River from the north. You see two barefooted men in shirtsleeves with their pants rolled up to their knees standing on the riverbank face-to-face, arguing loudly and pointing their fingers at each other. Both men look furious and have angry red faces. There are two wooden fishing rods nearby and a wooden bucket full of fish. "We agreed we would split our catch, you mealy-mouthed maggot!" one of them shouts. "You're only saying that because I caught six fish and you didn't catch any!" comes the angry reply from his friend. They stop arguing when they see you and reach for their swords. If you want to offer to buy their fish for 1 Gold Piece, turn to **162**. If you want to tell them that you are just passing by, turn to **186**.

278

After a short tussle, you land a pipefish. You take it back to your camp, where you cook it on a stick over an open fire and devour the tasty white flesh, what little of it there is. Add 1 *STAMINA* point. Knowing you need more than fish to eat in order to survive, you decide to explore the island. Turn to **116**.

279

The fletcher bids you farewell and holds out her hand. When you shake it, a violent pain shoots up your arm. Her face immediately lights up with evil glee, and she starts laughing hysterically. You try to pull your hand away but are unable to do so. Your hands are locked together in a cloud of swirling green mist which grows in size as the pain increases and spreads into your chest. Lose 2 *STAMINA* points.

"What a gullible fool you are," she sneers. "You actually believed me when I said I was Frances Fletcher. I'm afraid to say the real arrow maker had an unfortunate accident recently and is sadly no longer with us. My name is Gretta Morg. I am an assassin. The Death Hand pain you are experiencing will, I regret to say, lead to your heart stopping in a minute. Tonight, I will return to Port Blacksand with your head and claim the bounty of 1,000 Gold Pieces from Lord Azzur." If you were hurt by the Hand of Death on Snake Island, turn to **146**. If you did not touch the Hand of Death, turn to **379**.

280

You begin playing the flute but the tune that comes from it is nothing like the one you are trying to play. The magical melody makes the rats all scurry down the open drain in the middle of the cellar floor, screeching loudly. In less than a minute all the rats have disappeared. Add

1 *LUCK* point. You drag a heavy barrel over the drain to stop the rats coming out. You are about to go back upstairs when you hear a knock on the front door and hear Balthazar Wittle talk to somebody. "No, sorry, that's nobody I recognize. Goodbye." You hear the door shut and wonder who was there. Wittle appears at the top of the stairs and says, "There was a man by the name of Blackthorn at the door who showed me a 'Wanted' poster with your face on it. He was a quite fearsome-looking man in a wide-brimmed hat and a long brown coat. I told him I hadn't seen you. I've no idea what you have done, and I don't want to know, but it would appear that Lord Azzur wants your head! The tyrant held a banquet in Kaad last night for his cronies, and I heard he left this morning for Fang. He's gone to see his friend Baron Sukumvit, who is holding his annual Trial of Champions. Thank you for getting rid of the rats, but I suggest you leave now and go and sort out your differences with Blackthorn. He won't be far away." You thank Balthazar for his help and slip out of the front door, turning right up Clock Street. Turn to **89**.

281

"Friend or foe?" you ask sternly. The reply comes in the form of a dagger being thrown at you, although you cannot see it. *Test Your Luck*. If you are Lucky, turn to **156**. If you are Unlucky, turn to **220**.

You drop a Gold Piece on to the palm of Sidd's hand. "Thank you very much," he says, blinking rapidly. "By the way, I've just remembered it was actually yesterday when I had one egg for breakfast. I had two eggs this morning, which means of course that I'm happy to answer two questions! And since you have already paid me, I'll answer a second one for free." You ask him to tell you about the identity and whereabouts the nearest assassin. He holds the crystal ball aloft again on his fingertips and closes his eyes. Colourful gases swirl around inside when he speaks in his strange language. The gases quickly disperse again, and you see a tall warrior woman armed with a spear running along a dirt path at speed. She has striking silver markings covering much of her dark skin and her hair is close-cropped and dyed scarlet red. Sidd opens his eyes again as the image vanishes and says, "Ren-Ren Pakk is on her way to hunt you down. She is a Zengian Ultra, a fanatical fighter who is fleet of foot and has lightning reflexes. She will be a formidable opponent." You thank Sidd for the information and wish him farewell. Tall Tom says goodbye, telling you to come back again one day. You walk out of the tavern and think about which way to go. If you want to head north, turn to **133**. If you want to continue east, turn to **157**.

283

The Goblins have leather purses hanging over their shoulders on thin leather straps in which you find 3 Gold Pieces, six rough opals and a piece of torn paper with a notice printed on it. Unfortunately, some of the words are missing. All you can read is:

...will take place on the last day of this month and is open to all those who dare enter. The Trial of Champions requires that ye shall be of great courage and resolve, for only one contestant is permitted to survive.

By order of Baron Sukumvit of Fang

You pocket the Gold Pieces and set off again along the path, wondering when the Trial of Champions will be taking place. Turn to **244**.

284

One of the men follows you with his eyes as you walk past him, staring at you intently, and suddenly shouts out, "It's the murderer!" You don't stop to protest your innocence and you run off down the street as fast as you can. Turn to **314**.

285

You slide feet first into the burrow and push yourself down as far as you can. The Dragon loses sight of you and starts blasting the ground with balls of fire. But it soon tires and flies off east in search of prey elsewhere. You are about to crawl out of the tunnel when you hear yapping sounds coming from inside the burrow. You suddenly feel teeth biting your boots and kick out to free yourself. You scramble out and draw your sword to face three wiry-looking hounds with red eyes and slavering mouths whose den you have invaded. They are WORM DOGS, small and not very strong, but a single bite from one could be fatal since they are riddled with disease-carrying parasites. You must fight them one at a time.

	SKILL	STAMINA
First WORM DOG	4	4
Second WORM DOG	5	3
Third WORM DOG	4	5

If you win without losing an *Attack Round*, turn to **177**. If you win, but lose one or more *Attack Rounds*, turn to **50**.

286

You watch the Orc put a hunting horn to his lips and give it a long blast. You hear a roar from the band of Orcs, and soon there are twenty angry Orcs gathered around the base of the tree looking up at you, snarling and shouting. Their leader barks out an order and two Orcs start chopping at the tree with their axes. You hear the sound of splintering wood and watch the Orcs become excited when the tree creaks and begins to topple over. You land heavily on the ground and before you can stand up to defend yourself, you are beaten to a pulp by cudgels and clubs. Your adventure is over.

287

The woman curses and says in a sneering voice, "You are right to be suspicious of me, stranger. I am not Frances Fletcher. The arrow maker had an unfortunate accident recently and is sadly no longer with us. My name is Gretta Morg. I am an assassin. Let us engage in combat but, in the time-honoured tradition of the Scorpion Guild, let us shake hands first before blood is spilled." If you want to shake Gretta Morg's hand, turn to **126**. If you would rather answer her with your sword, turn to **60**.

Their fierce eyes firmly fixed on you

288

You walk through the open gate of a high-fenced boatyard. There are several wooden boats propped up on wooden piles in the yard in various states of repair. Some are having holes in their hulls repaired and others are just being painted. You see a man in a green tunic standing on a ladder, leaning against a small fishing boat. He has a large brush in his hand and is busy varnishing the hull. On seeing you he climbs slowly down the ladder and lets out a high-pitched whistle, whereupon two vicious-looking dogs come bounding into the yard. They run over to the man and sit down at his feet, panting, their fierce eyes firmly fixed on you. "How can I help?" the man asks casually. If you want to ask him if he's interested in buying a boat, turn to **380**. If you want to ask him if he knows of a man called Garanka Vassell, turn to **102**.

289

The giant scarlet-coloured Dragon catches sight of you, and swoops down to blast you with its fiery breath. If you are carrying a shield, turn to **196**. If you do not have a shield, turn to **206**.

290

One of the pirates throws a rope down to you, yelling at you to climb on board. You are greeted by the captain, a rough-looking bearded man with an eye patch and a gold tooth. Surrounded by his men, he points his pistol at you and says, "Welcome on board. You'll be pleased to know that I'm a generous man, and I'm going to give you two choices. One, you give me everything you have and join my crew, or two, I kill you!" All his men start laughing and cheering, yelling at you to choose option two. If you want to surrender your possessions to the captain and join his crew, turn to **199**. If you would rather draw your sword and fight, turn to **168**.

291

Bobby's eyes light up at the mention of the word "assassin". He looks at his brother and says, "Brother Billy, didn't an assassin come knocking on our door yesterday asking if we'd seen the murderer on his 'Wanted' poster?"

"He most definitely did, brother Bobby. Now where did I put that poster?"

"It's in your back pocket, pea brain!"

"So it is. Let's have a look at it," Billy says excitedly. Holding it at arm's length, Billy squints, trying to focus on the poster. He then brings it up close to his nose and starts cursing to himself. His brother snatches the poster from him and looks at it closely with his eyes scrunched up into tiny slits. "Bah, it's all too blurry. I can't focus my old eyes," Bobby blurts out in frustration. He turns the poster towards you and, tapping the face on it with a fat finger, says, "You down there, is this you?" If you want to reply that the person on the poster is you, turn to **349**. If you want to say it isn't you, turn to **300**.

292

The storekeeper rummages through all the drawers and shelves in his store but comes up empty-handed. "Sorry, I must have sold the last pair," he says with a shrug of the shoulders. If you want to buy some Provisions, turn to **64**. If you would rather leave the store and head east on foot, turn to **203**.

293

The woman slips through the crowd and runs down an alleyway up ahead on the left side of the street. You follow her down the alleyway, and immediately right under a stone archway and down a narrow passageway separating two old brick buildings. The woman suddenly stops and turns, and you see that the expression on her face has turned from being friendly to evil. Her piercing green eyes are firmly fixed on yours, and you feel unable to look away. You try to draw your sword, but your head starts to spin, making it hard to focus. "My name is Red Ruth and I too belong to the Scorpion Guild of Assassins. You are trapped by my Mind Control powers," she says coldly as she pulls out a long knife from inside her cloak. "I will be well rewarded for the gift I will deliver to Lord Azzur." If you are wearing a copper headband, turn to **344**. If you are not wearing a headband, turn to **158**.

294

You are about two-thirds of the way down the side of the cliff when one of the steps comes loose underfoot. *Test Your Luck*. If you are Lucky, turn to **112**. If you are Unlucky, turn to **27**.

295

With their leader dead, the other Wolves run off into the long grass, yelping loudly. You continue your walk north and eventually come to the edge of the forest. It is a dark and foreboding forest with ancient gnarled trees and no doubt gruesome creatures lying in wait. "I wouldn't enter the Forest of Fiends if I were you," a voice calls out from above. "You might never come out." You look up and see a man no more than a metre high standing on a branch of an oak tree. He is wearing a floppy hat and a brown shirt. "Give me some food and I'll give you some advice," he says jovially. If you want to give the little man some of your Provisions, turn to **202**. If you would rather decline his offer and enter the forest, turn to **51**.

296

You tell the pirate to sit down and be quiet or else you will kick him overboard. Aware that the sea monster might reappear at any moment, you trim the sail and set a course. If you want to head due east towards the Red River estuary, turn to **345**. If you would rather sail southeast to Port Blacksand, turn to **393**.

297

There is a sign above the door of the hut which says FANG FERRY. You open the door to find a man slumped in a wooden chair lying face down on a table in a pool of blood with a dagger sticking out of his back. There is a message on the table written in blood with his finger which says, *Get Zeedle*. But it is too late to save the ferryman. You look outside to see the man in the rowing boat is still asleep and decide to ring the brass bell to wake him up. Turn to **39**.

298

You walk on, unaware that the woman has turned around to follow you. She creeps up on you silently from behind and, without warning, smashes you on the back of the head with a large stone. Lose 2 *STAMINA* points. You stagger forward, trying to clear your head. You manage to turn round to face her and she grabs your hand. You feel a shocking pain run up your arm and through your body which makes your heart beat uncomfortably quickly. Your hand is locked in hers, enveloped in a cloud of translucent green mist. The pain increases and becomes unbearable, but you are unable to pull your hand away. The woman tightens her grip and starts to laugh hysterically. Lose 2 *STAMINA* points. "What a fool you are," she sneers. "Never turn your back on an assassin! My name is Gretta Morg of the Scorpion Guild of Assassins. The Death Hand pain you are experiencing will, I regret to say, lead to your heart stopping in a minute. Tonight, I will return to Port Blacksand with your head and claim the bounty of 1,000 Gold Pieces from Lord Azzur." If you were harmed by the Hand of Death on Snake Island, turn to **146**. If you did not touch the Hand of Death, turn to **379**.

299

The second finger of the skeleton hand is easier to prise away than the first. It snaps like a dry twig, which lifts your spirits and gives you the mental strength to snap off the remaining fingers. The fingerless hand falls to the ground, and you stamp down hard on it, crushing it underfoot, which causes the smoke cloud to disperse. You drop to your knees, exhausted and gasping for air. Lose 2 *STAMINA* points. Turn to **223**.

300

Billy looks annoyed and says, "That's not the answer I wanted. Methinks you are of no use to us. So, it's time to say goodbye with a game of Beat-the-Buss. These are the rules, so listen carefully. Brother Bobby and I are going to climb on to the roof. I should tell you he's got a blunderbuss. That's where the buss in Beat-the-Buss comes from, as in blunderbuss, if you're understanding me? I'm going to throw you a rope and count to twenty before brother Bobby starts shooting. All you have to do is climb out and hightail it for the wooden gate without being shot full of lead. Are you understanding me? Don't try any funny business or brother Bobby will shoot you right here and now." The brothers disappear and seconds later a thick length of rope drops down into the cellar. You catch hold of it and give it a tug. Satisfied it will bear your weight, you haul yourself out of the cellar. There is a ladder leading up to a skylight in the roof, through which you hear a voice counting, "Twelve . . . thirteen . . . fourteen. . ." and realize you must run for your life. You bolt for the door and run out of the farmhouse and down the path as fast as you can. If you are wearing Elven Boots, turn to **90**. If you are not wearing Elven Boots, turn to **323**.

301

A look of sheer terror spreads across the man's face when you draw your sword, and he retreats slowly until his back is up against the wall. "I'm sorry, I wasn't being serious about you having to pay me," he says nervously. "In fact, let me give you another bottle of apple juice for your troubles. You seemed to enjoy the first one." He sees you frown at the mention of apple juice. "Ah yes, let me explain. My healing potion is actually apple juice. I must also confess that the apples I put on the table back there weren't poisonous either. I was just trying to think of new ways to make money from my apples. I have so many I don't know what to do with them all. It's all I can do to give them away. I now realize the poisoned apple ruse was not such a good idea. Sorry." You put your sword away and the man looks at you sheepishly and hands you a bottle of apple juice from his cupboard. You take it from him and gulp down the refreshing juice. Add 1 *STAMINA* point. If you want to give him a coin in payment anyway, turn to **151**. If you want to leave the hut and carry on walking east, turn to **277**.

302

The captain helps you gather wood to make a fire and produces some salted beef and dried fruit from his boat. "Just in case you are hungry," he says with a grin, handing you the food. You enjoy a fine meal keeping warm by the fire and talking to the captain about Lord Azzur. Add 2 *STAMINA* points. It begins to rain hard, and with a cold wind whipping up, you retire to the hut for the night, taking it in turns to be on watch in case of unexpected visitors. You wake early the next morning to find the sun shining through the window to the sound of waves gently lapping on the beach. The captain is already on his boat, checking his gear and filling a barrel with fresh rainwater. A good breeze and a calm sea bodes well for a quick passage to the mainland. "I'm just going to see if I can find a piece of wood to make a new tiller for the rudder," the captain says on seeing you. "The old one is split, and we don't want to be out at sea without being able to steer the boat! I'll be back soon." The captain heads off, leaving you to gather up your possessions, including Oleander Redfly's bow and quiver of arrows, which all have flights made of black feathers. You also take Redfly's prized weapon, her shimmering Astral Sword. Add 1 *SKILL* point. An hour passes, but the captain has still not returned, so you decide to go in search of him. You follow his footprints deep into the undergrowth and it isn't long before you find him. His limbs are held fast by thick vines, and the poor man is in terrible pain caused by a long tendril thrust down his throat. He has fallen foul of Hell's Bloodwort, a giant carnivorous plant. The Bloodwort snares its victims with its long vines which wrap around limbs like giant snakes, making escape virtually impossible. With its prey unable to move, a Bloodwort will force its long, proboscis-like tendril down a victim's throat to suck their blood from inside their body. The terrified captain appears doomed, and his muffled screams turn your blood cold. If you want to attack the Bloodwort to rescue the captain, turn to **43**. If you would rather run back to the beach, turn to **275**.

303

The man brings his horse to a halt. He looks you up and down and says in a gruff voice, "I'm headed north-east. For 2 Gold Pieces I'll take you to the log cabin that's about an hour's ride from here. Yes or no?" If you want to ride with the horseman, turn to **153**. If you want to decline his offer and set off on foot, turn to **252**.

304

By now, the ship is almost on its side, and everything on deck that is not lashed down spills overboard. The pirate ship is beginning to break up, and there is nothing the pirates can do to stop it. Pulling yourself along the wooden deck rail hand-over-hand is exhausting, but you finally reach the stern. You waste no time and cut the tow rope with the cleaver and jump into the sea. When you surface, you see that the *Blue Moon* has drifted away some distance. You swim as hard as you can towards your boat and see that another pirate has the same idea. You hear the sound of the ship's mast breaking behind you, followed by the unnerving sound of bubbling air escaping from the upturned hull as it is dragged underwater by the giant sea monster. The pirate reaches the *Blue Moon* before you and scrambles on board. He starts to trim the flapping sail, determined to get away from the Kraken as quickly as possible. You call out to him to wait for you, but he ignores you. The only thing you can do is to throw your meat cleaver at him, a difficult shot whilst bobbing up and down on the open sea. Roll two dice. If the number rolled is less than or equal to your *SKILL* score, turn to **7**. If the number rolled is greater than your *SKILL* score, turn to **119**.

305

You open the door just wide enough to look outside and are relieved to find that the Orcs are nowhere to be seen. You slip outside, closing the bark-covered door behind you, which fits into the trunk so snugly that nobody would know it was there. You make your way northwards through the trees to where the wood opens out on to a huge grass-covered plain where you see two paths. One path heads north towards a forest and the other leads off it and heads north-east towards a town in the far distance. If you want to follow the path north towards the forest, turn to **101**. If you want to follow the path north to the junction and turn north-east towards the town, turn to **200**.

306

The Decayer is a slow-moving but very dangerous creature. You must try to avoid it spitting on you since its acidic drool will burn you badly on contact with your skin. Your head is spinning from the noxious smell coming from its body, inhibiting your ability to fight. Reduce your *SKILL* by 2 points for this battle.

DECAYER   *SKILL 8*   *STAMINA 8*

Each time the Decayer wins an *Attack Round*, lose 4 STAMINA points. If you win, turn to **97**.

307

As you approach the outskirts of Kaad, the path widens into a dirt road leading to the main entrance gates of town. You see a horse-drawn open carriage coming out through the gates driven by a man wearing a bowler hat and a tailored waistcoat over his crisp white shirt. Sitting bolt upright next to him, looking snootily down her nose with an air of grand superiority, is a rosy-cheeked woman wearing a floral hat and long baggy black dress. If you want to put your hand up to stop the carriage to talk to the woman, turn to **120**. If you want to keep your head down and enter Kaad, turn to **390**.

308

You manage to wriggle out from underneath the rope net before the Goblin has reached the ground. The Goblins are furious that you have escaped from their trap and leap forward to attack you with their short swords. Fight them one at a time.

	SKILL	STAMINA
First GOBLIN	5	6
Second GOBLIN	5	5

If you win, turn to **283**.

It is Baron Sukumvit himself

309

You walk through the main gates, where colourful flags and bunting are hanging from all the buildings. There is a wild carnival atmosphere in town with everybody enjoying the Trial of Champions festivities. The streets are packed with people singing and dancing to the sounds of flutes, pipes and drums. When they see you arrive with Throm, the cheering crowd parts to make a path for you to walk to the Town Hall to register your entry. The officials warn you that your chances of surviving "The Walk", as it is known, are virtually nil, and you tell them that you understand. A violet scarf is tied to your arm and you are taken to a luxurious guest house, where you spend the rest of the day resting and recuperating. The next morning a servant takes you to the entrance of Deathtrap Dungeon, where five warriors are standing proudly in line, waving to the jubilant crowd. Throm is one of them. You nod at him and he acknowledges you with just the slightest movement of his head. Standing on a gold podium surrounded by Guards is a long, white-bearded man wearing lavish red robes and an enormous headdress. It is Baron Sukumvit himself, the Overlord of Fang and owner of the Deathtrap Dungeon. Standing just behind him is a formidable-looking figure whose face and body is totally concealed by clothing apart from his cold, ice-blue eyes. He is wearing a hooded cloak made of dark blue silk with gold fastenings and a thick gold chain around his neck with a golden scorpion hanging from it. His face is hidden by long strips of blue silk wrapped tightly around his head, held in place by an emerald brooch on his forehead and a large golden scorpion brooch on his head. "Lord Azzur," you whisper to yourself. If you want to wait to be introduced to Baron Sukumvit, turn to **233**. If you want to leap on to the podium to attack Lord Azzur, turn to **65**.

310

With a strong easterly breeze helping, your voyage to Port Blacksand is quick and trouble free. The familiar rugged buildings of Port Blacksand come into view and it's not long before you are moored up alongside the harbour wall of the old port, notorious for the pirates, cutthroats and thieves who live there. Two rough-looking thugs with missing teeth and stubbly beards are standing on the quay, watching you closely, and start whispering to each other. It's only a few days since you were last here, but now everything has changed, and you can't afford to trust anybody. If you want to ask them if they know of anybody who might want to buy your boat, turn to **48**. If you want to walk past them and enter the Black Lobster Tavern at the end of the quay, turn to **334**.

311

You stand over the fallen Orc breathing hard, but there is no time to search the body. You make your way quickly north to get as far away as you can from the Orcs before they realize what has happened. Just when you think you have escaped, a long blast on a hunting horn signals that you have been spotted by one of their scouts. You hear a loud roar behind you and the thunder of heavy footsteps of the band of Orcs giving chase. All you can do is run. If you are wearing Elven Boots, turn to **241**. If you are wearing ordinary leather boots, turn to **18**.

312

The archer's aim is deadly accurate. An arrow sinks into your leg with a sickening thud. Lose 2 *STAMINA* points. Your attacker reloads and fires again, and you are hit a second time, this time in the midriff. Lose 1 *SKILL* point and roll one die and reduce your *STAMINA* by the number rolled. If you are still alive, turn to **348**.

313

When you touch her hand, a violent pain shoots up your arm. Her face lights up with evil glee, and she starts to laugh hysterically. You try to pull your hand away but are unable to do so. Your hands are locked together in a cloud of translucent green mist which grows in size and increases the pain which spreads to your chest. Lose 2 *STAMINA* points. "What a gullible fool you are to believe I am Frances Fletcher," she sneers. "I'm afraid to say the real arrow maker had an unfortunate accident recently and is sadly no longer with us. My name is Gretta Morg. I am an assassin. The Death Hand pain you are experiencing will cause your heart to stop in a minute. Tonight, I will return to Port Blacksand with your head and claim the bounty of 1,000 Gold Pieces from Lord Azzur." If you were harmed by the Hand of Death on Snake Island, turn to **146**. If you didn't touch the Hand of Death, turn to **379**.

314

You run away from the crowd as fast as you can with their alarm calls echoing down the street. Four ARMED GUARDS run out of a building and block the street up ahead, and you have no choice but to charge at them. You manage to slay one of the Guards before the crowd catches up and joins the fray. A blow to your head from a wooden club sends you crashing to the floor. Two of the Guards grab your arms and the other Guard takes your sword. Your feet are shackled, and you are dragged away to the cheers of the crowd. You are thrown in a dungeon cell, where you are chained to a wall to await the arrival of the Earl of Kaad who, you are told, will decide whether or not to hand you over to Lord Azzur. When the Earl finally arrives, you can tell from the stern faces of the Guards behind him that it is not good news. Your worst fears are confirmed when he tells you solemnly that you will be taken in chains to Executioner's Square in Port Blacksand. Your adventure is over.

315

You swing your sword through the darkness, and feel it strike home. A man's muffled cry breaks the silence, and you hear the intruder stumble backwards. You step forward and strike again. Although injured, the intruder is a skilful KNIFE FIGHTER who is very agile and light on his feet. You must fight him in total darkness!

KNIFE FIGHTER	*SKILL 7*	*STAMINA 6*

If you win, turn to **174**.

316

The woman shuts the door quickly behind her just as the Orcs appear on the top of the hill. The bark-covered door fits into the trunk so snugly that nobody would know it was there. You run on with the Orcs charging down the hill after you in hot pursuit. You weave your way through the trees, dashing quickly through the wood thanks to your Elven Boots. Unable to catch you, the Orcs give up their chase and start fighting between themselves again. The wood eventually opens out on to a huge grass-covered plain where you see two paths. One path heads north towards a forest and the other leads off it and heads north-east towards a town in the distance. If you want to take the path north towards the forest, turn to **101**. If you want to follow this path as far as the junction and take the new path towards the town, turn to **200**.

317

The storekeeper shakes his head and says, "I don't think I've got a pair of Elven Boots in stock, but let me have a look, you never know." *Test Your Luck*. If you are Lucky, turn to **170**. If you are Unlucky, turn to **292**.

318

You slide the gold band up your sword arm and over your bicep. It fits perfectly but it feels like it is burning your skin. If you want to keep it on, turn to **57**. If you would rather take it off and place it in your backpack, turn to **139**.

319

You shake the purse and hear what sounds like coins rattling inside. You loosen the leather string tie and empty out 12 Gold Pieces on to the palm of your hand. Add 1 *LUCK* point. You happily pocket the coins and decide what to do. If you have not done so already, you can either open the silver box (turn to **377**) or close the chest and scour the beach in the hope of finding something of interest (turn to **231**).

320

You jump on to a barrel near the wall. One of the Giant Rats leaps up and sinks its sharp teeth into your boot just as the chasing crowd enters the alleyway led by four ARMED GUARDS. You try kicking out to shake the Rat off your boot, but only succeed in making the barrel wobble. *Test Your Luck*. If you are Lucky, turn to **212**. If you are Unlucky, turn to **72**.

321

You see that the woman was wearing the same silver necklace and scorpion pendant as the other assassins who tried to kill you. You take it from her neck and put it in your pocket. You also help yourself to her arrows and 2 Gold Pieces in her pocket before setting off east again, wondering how many more assassins you will have to face before this nightmare is over. Turn to **45**.

322

The ring fits perfectly on your middle finger. Minutes later it begins to feel very tight on your finger. You try to take it off but are unable to do so. It continues to tighten, causing your finger to turn purple and go completely numb. There was a reason why your attacker was not wearing the ring, and now there is nothing you can do to take it off. The ring is cursed. Lose 1 *SKILL* point, 1 *STAMINA* point and 2 *LUCK* points. You begin your quest for food on the third day feeling annoyed with yourself. Turn to **11**.

323

You hear a loud bang behind you and feel a terrible pain in the back of your leg, which has been peppered by lead shot.

Lose 4 *STAMINA* points. If you are still alive, you stagger on with a burning pain in your leg and manage to reach the farmhouse gate before Bobby has time to fire again. You turn around to see the twins sitting on the roof, with Bobby holding his blunderbuss in the air, a wisp of white smoke drifting out of the barrel. They give you the thumbs up and begin laughing so hard that they almost fall off the roof. You decide it best to leave them to it and bandage your leg before heading for Kaad. Turn to **307**.

324

You hand over the Elven Boots to the Gnome, who quickly kicks off his old boots and pulls the new ones on. He stands up and runs around in a circle at high speed, clapping his hands with glee. He gives you 10 Gold Pieces and asks you where you are going. You reply that you are heading north. "Well, if you haven't been there before, you should definitely visit Kaad since it's on your way. You won't forget it. Most people who live there are pig-poo crazy, and some of them are as mad as a box of frogs!" You thank the Gnome for his advice and set off again. Turn to **179**.

325

The Dragon loses sight of you under the cover of the thick foliage of the trees and starts blasting the ground randomly with balls of fire, hoping to hit you. But it soon tires and flies off east in search of prey elsewhere. With the coast clear, you head west back to your hut on the other side of the island. Turn to **217**.

326

You reach down to loosen your attacker's silk neckerchief, and your suspicions are quickly confirmed when you see the silver necklace and scorpion pendant around his neck. You break the chain and place the pendant in your pocket. A search of the assassin's pockets yields 1 Gold Piece and a small bottle of deadly poison which you decide to keep. You leave the gardens and walk left along Fountain Street as far as the junction with Bell Street. There is a large group of people up ahead, some of them armed with clubs and pitchforks, who you suspect might be looking for you. Your time in Kaad has been a battle for survival, and rather than risk getting into any more fights, you turn right into Bell Street and head for the main gates, trying to avoid attention as you hurry along. Bell Street runs into Clock Street, which leads you to the market square and on down Crown Street and the main gates. There aren't many people about other than a few merchants leaving town after a long day at the market. As you walk out through the gates, a mean-looking man in a hooded black cloak and a bow and quiver of arrows slung over his shoulder rides past you on a black horse. He glances down at you as he passes by and spits on the ground. If you want to ask him for a ride, turn to **303**. If you want to carry on walking, turn to **252**.

327

The general store is a large wooden building set back from the river some twenty metres. It has wide steps leading up to a porch where there are several wooden barrels and two rocking chairs. A glazed wooden door leads into the store itself. You bound up the steps but are stopped in your tracks when you see a "Wanted" poster on the wall by the door with your face drawn on it. If you still want to enter the store, turn to **23**. If you would rather not risk going in, and head east on foot instead, turn to **203**.

328

You walk east along the edge of the forest, mindful of any creatures lurking in the shadows. An hour later you see the skyline of Kaad only a short distance beyond the forest. Looking south, you see a wide expanse of grasslands which form the westernmost part of the Pagan Plains. Whilst you are surveying the land, you do not notice a large Spider drop down on to your shoulder from the tree you are standing under. Suddenly you feel something on your neck. *Test Your Luck*. If you are Lucky, turn to **256**. If you are Unlucky, turn to **210**.

329

You slip over the side of the boat and grab hold of the rudder, keeping your head down as low to the water as possible to avoid being seen. The loose sail starts to flap around noisily in the wind. You hear voices coming from the pirate ship with the crew arguing about how the *Blue Moon* came to be drifting at sea with nobody on board. A gruff voice suddenly barks out an order: "Shut up, you dogs! One of you throw out a grappling hook and pull that boat in! We'll tow it to Port Blacksand and sell it." You hear the iron hook land on the boat and catch under the bench seat on the foredeck. Your boat is pulled to the back of the pirate ship, where it is tied on before turning for Port Blacksand. You find yourself being dragged along at speed, and it is all you can do to hang on. If you want to give yourself up to the pirates, turn to **290**. If you want to climb back on board the *Blue Moon* and hope you are not seen, turn to **385**.

330

The passageway leads into Bell Street, which is lined on both sides with old houses and shops. Looking left, you see that the street ends at a junction. Looking right, you see a crossroads where there are some people standing around talking. If you want to go left up Bell Street, turn to **123**. If you want to walk towards the crossroads, turn to **226**.

331

You sling the coil of rope over your shoulder and walk over to the cupboard at the back of the cave. Turn to **187**.

332

You have stepped on an animal trap, but luckily your foot didn't trigger the spring holding the jagged iron jaws apart. You decide to spring the trap with the tip of your sword and render it useless. You continue on your way and eventually come to a rickety old gate on the right which has a large sign nailed to it with the words BOGG FARM – BOG OFF painted on it. A gravel path leads from the gate to an old farmhouse, which sits in the middle of a small field separated from the grassland by a wooden fence. There is a stone post next to the gate with an arrow carved on it pointing towards the town and the words KAAD – 1 MILE underneath. From this distance, Kaad looks like it is a small town. The buildings are few in number and are mostly one or two storeys high except a stone tower in the centre of town. If you want to open the gate and walk up the path to the farmhouse, turn to **70**. If you would rather continue on to Kaad, turn to **307**.

333

You tap the man on the shoulder, which wakes him up with a start. "Whoa!" he says, leaping to his feet. "Thief! Robber! Help! What do you want? I've got nothing worth stealing. I'm just a poor apple grower," he splutters out, trembling. You calm him down and tell him you just want to buy a Potion of Healing. "Ah, I see. I'm afraid I don't have any healing potions. My so-called healing potion is actually apple juice. And I should say that the apples I put on the table back there weren't poisonous either. I was just trying to think of new ways to make money from my apples. I have so many I don't know what to do with them. It's all I can do to give them away. I now realize the poisoned apple ruse was not such a good idea. But I'm penniless and desperate. I'd be very grateful if you would buy a bottle of my apple juice. It's quite delicious. A Gold Piece would be very generous of you, but a silver coin would do." The man picks up the bottle of apple juice and hands it to you, looking sheepish. You take it from him and gulp down the tasty contents. Add 1 *STAMINA* point. If you want to pay him, turn to **151**. If you want to leave the hut and carry on walking east, turn to **277**.

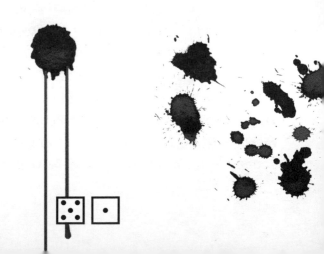

334

The Black Lobster is like most taverns in Port Blacksand, full of pickpockets, crooks, thieves, tricksters, card sharps and charlatans looking to relieve drunken sailors, boat builders and fishermen of their money. When you open the door, your nostrils are assaulted by an unpleasant mix of old ale, stale body odour and cheap perfume. The tavern is buzzing with activity. Behind the wooden bar stands a stern-looking giant of a man wearing a dirty apron over his white vest who goes by the name of Grim. He has large gold earrings in both ears, and his chest and arms are covered in tattoos. The innkeeper eyes you suspiciously as you approach the bar, where you see a "Wanted" poster pinned on the wall behind him. If you want to talk to the innkeeper, turn to **367**. If you would rather talk to the barmaid who is walking towards you laden with mugs of ale, turn to **149**.

335

The old woman nods enthusiastically when you take off your boots and signals her approval by giving you a thumbs up. You wave back at her and walk on barefooted, following the map down Quiet Street to where it ends at a T-junction. You put your boots back on and turn right into Fountain Street to walk to the Public Gardens up ahead on the left. Turn to **268**.

336

The bees continue to sting you as you scramble down the tree. Lose 2 *STAMINA* points. You run back through the undergrowth as fast as you can until you reach the cliff edge once more. Your face is puffed up with the angry welts caused by the bee stings, blurring your vision. Lose 1 *SKILL* point. The pain is unbearable, but there is no time to lose. You must chance running down the steps to the beach to escape the bees. *Test Your Luck*. If you are Lucky, turn to **248**. If you are Unlucky, turn to **272**.

337

You find it impossible to breathe as the bony fingers sink deeper into your throat. With your windpipe blocked, your face turns deep red. Try as you might, you are unable to dislodge the skeleton hand from your throat. You soon pass out and never regain consciousness. Your adventure is over.

338

The man glares at you, and says, "You're lying. Old Sam never played cards. He didn't know how to. I'm guessing you stole his boat. I've got no time for the likes of you. Be off with you or I'll set my dogs on you." The vicious-looking dogs sense the mood of their owner turning sour and start snarling and barking loudly. Not wishing to get into an unnecessary fight, you set off east on foot at a brisk pace. Turn to **203**.

339

Otto tells you not to worry if you hear any sounds in the night. The creatures outside will not be able to get inside the cabin. After paying Otto, you retire to your room, locking the door behind you. You place a chair against the door handle to make extra sure nobody can enter before finally flopping on top of the bed and falling into a deep sleep. You wake early the next morning and look out of the window to view the scrubland of the Pagan Plain, which stretches out as far as you can see. You go downstairs, where Otto is laying a table for breakfast. He turns to you and says, "Would bread, butter, cheese, jam and a jug of water be to your satisfaction?" You nod in approval and are soon enjoying a hearty breakfast in preparation for the new day. Add 2 *STAMINA* points. When you are about to leave, Otto asks you where you are headed to. You reply that you are on your way to Fang. "Not another one!" he says jovially. "It's that time of the year, I guess. The best way to go is to follow the trail just north of here, which will take you to the ferryman, who will row you across the River Kok for 1 Gold Piece. I wouldn't risk swimming across if I were you." You thank Otto for his hospitality and set off at a brisk pace. You soon pick up the trail and press on, eager to reach Fang by noon. Turn to **378**.

340

You soon realize that there are just too many of them to fight if you want to live to see another day. You cut two of them down, but another pirate slashes your arm with his cutlass. Lose 2 *STAMINA* points. You have no choice but to jump over the back of the boat and swim to the *Blue Moon*. Turn to **24**.

He has a large nose and particularly large ears

341

You walk through the open door of the tavern, wary of any unexpected surprises. There is a stairwell straight ahead, down which Garanka Vassell came running only moments ago. To your right there is a large bar room with just a solitary customer sitting at a table drinking from a pewter mug. He is a thin man in ragged clothing with wiry hair sticking out in every direction. He looks at you for a moment, and then looks away. Behind the bar stands a very tall man in a brightly patterned waistcoat. He has a large nose and particularly large ears. He places his hands on the bar, leans forward, and says in a stern voice, "I saw what happened out there. It's all very well for you to go killing off an evil assassin, but he was a customer of mine. Who is going to pay me for his room? Somebody owes me 2 Gold Pieces and that somebody is going to have to be you! If you pay Vassell's bill, I'll give you a bit of advice for your trouble." Will you:

Pay 2 Gold Pieces to Tall Tom?	Turn to **26**
Leave the tavern and head north?	Turn to **133**
Leave the tavern and continue east?	Turn to **157**

342

Before you are able to untangle yourself from the net, the second Goblin jumps down from the tree to join his accomplice. You feel a blow to the back of your head and slump to the ground unconscious. Lose 2 *STAMINA* points. When you wake up sometime later, you discover that all your Gold Pieces have been taken, and the Goblins are nowhere to be seen. Lose 1 *LUCK* point. You pick yourself up and set off east along the path, nursing a pounding headache. Turn to **244**.

343

As soon as you touch the skeleton hand, it flies off the nail and grips you by the throat with its bony fingers squeezing hard on your windpipe, making you gasp for air. The more you try to pull it off, the tighter it grips your throat. Arcane magic from a spell cast long ago gave the Hand of Death its deadly powers. Lose 1 *SKILL* point, 1 LUCK point and 2 *STAMINA* points. Roll two dice. If the number rolled is less than or equal to your *SKILL* score, turn to **159**. If the number rolled is greater than your *SKILL* score, turn to **46**.

344

Your dizziness stops as quickly as it started. The copper headband you are wearing is an ancient Mind Shield artefact which blocks Red Ruth's mental powers. She curses when she sees you recover and draw your sword. Howling with anger, she lunges forward to strike you with her long knife. You must fight the Assassin!

RED RUTH   *SKILL 5*   *STAMINA 5*

If you win, turn to **33**.

345

Apart from Blood Sharks circling you at one point, the voyage to the mainland passes without incident. A strong easterly wind ensures a swift passage, and a few hours later the rugged Allansian coastline comes into view. The cliffs are quite high, but you see an estuary directly ahead which you recognize as the entrance to Red River. You don't speak to the pirate during the voyage, and it's only when you get close to land that you tell him that you are going to set him free, even though he does not deserve it. You untie him and tell him to swim to the shore. He protests, but you boot him overboard and sail on. You are soon at the mouth of the river, where you see two wooden buildings on the northern bank. You steer the *Blue Moon* over to the bank and jump out. It feels great to be back on dry land, but you are also very aware that Lord Azzur has his best assassins hunting you down, looking to relieve you of your head. If only Captain Crow had told you who the other assassins were before he died, you would have been better prepared. Now everybody you meet could be the next assassin for all you know. But at least you should recognize Garanka Vassell when you see him. You walk towards the buildings, which you note are a boatyard and a general store. Thinking you might be able to sell the *Blue Moon*, you decide to visit the boatyard first. Turn to **288**.

346

You slide the ring on to your finger and feel a tingling sensation in your hand. You are wearing a Ring of Fortune. *Test Your Luck*. If you are Lucky, turn to **218**. If you are Unlucky, turn to **273**.

347

You salute the Baron with gritted teeth and walk over to the entrance of the dungeon to take your place alongside your fellow contestants. Turn to **400**.

348

Grimacing with pain, you pull the arrows from your leg and chest. You grit your teeth and draw your sword, and limp over to fight your attacker, who throws back her hood to reveal the unmistakable features of a DARK ELF PRIESTESS. Her neck is covered with tattoos of writhing serpents and her long ice-white hair is tied up high on her head. She is wearing studded leather armour with iron-plated shoulder pads. Staring at you with cold, amethyst-blue eyes, she draws her long sword slowly from its scabbard, a shimmering blade made of the finest Salamonian steel enveloped in a swirling mist of vivid colours. Swinging it skilfully above her head, the Dark Elf advances towards you, meeting your sword with a clash of steel, her chilling war cry sending a shiver down your spine.

DARK ELF PRIESTESS   *SKILL 8*   *STAMINA 8*

If you win, turn to **61**.

349

Bobby slaps his thigh and says, "Ka-boom! I think we've struck gold, brother Billy! That assassin said he would pay us 10 Gold Pieces if we caught the villain he was looking for. Go out to the back yard and ring the brass bell three times like he told you to." Bobby pulls the trapdoor back up and bolts it shut, and you find yourself in total darkness again. You hear the shrill sound of a bell ring out three times. All you can do is draw your sword and wait to see what happens. Some fifteen minutes later the trapdoor drops down and you see three people looking down at you – the Bogg brothers and a long-haired BARBARIAN who is wearing a fur cloak over leather armour and brandishing two double-edged axes made of polished steel. "You did well, boys," the Barbarian says in a deep voice.

"When are you going to pay us?" asks Billy.

"I'm not going to pay you! The bounty will be mine. Dax the Axe shares his spoils with no one."

"Well, that's not fair," Billy says angrily. "And we don't take kindly to people who are mean to us."

Bobby suddenly produces a blunderbuss from out of the rubbish pile and points it at the assassin. "You've got five seconds to jump into the cellar or I'll let you have it, and I promise you things get a bit messy at this range. One . . . two . . . three. . ." The Barbarian sneers and leaps down into the cellar, landing perfectly on his feet. He roars in anger and swings his axes at you.

DAX THE AXE   SKILL 9   STAMINA 8

If you win, turn to **103**.

350

You flinch on seeing a puff of white smoke shoot out of the barrel of the pistol. At such short range, the captain cannot miss. The lead ball hits you in the midriff, with the force knocking you over. Lose 1 *SKILL* point. Roll two dice and reduce your *STAMINA* by the total. If you are still alive, turn to **81**.

351

You pay the storekeeper 5 Gold Pieces, pull on the new boots, and pack away your old boots. You walk outside and run a short distance and are amazed how fast you can run. You go back inside the store, where the storekeeper is waiting for you with a smile on his face. "Believe me now, do you? Before you march off in your new boots, you might like to buy some food. You look like you are very hungry. I make the best bread in the land, and stock the best cheese and tomatoes you have ever tasted. I'll sell you a fresh loaf, a big chunk of cheese and some ripe tomatoes for just 1 Gold Piece. If you need something special to put the food in, I'll also sell you a wizard's backpack for a bargain price of 4 Gold Pieces. It's a rare Bag of Everything. No matter what you put in it, it will always feel as light as a feather." Will you:

Buy the food for 1 Gold Piece?	Turn to **105**
Buy the food and the backpack for 5 Gold Pieces?	Turn to **364**
Decline his offer?	Turn to **215**

352

You manage to slay one of the Guards but are overwhelmed by the sheer weight of numbers of the crowd. The blow from a wooden club to your head sends you crashing to the floor. You are lying sprawled out in the rubbish, dazed and confused. Two of the Guards grab your arms and the other one takes your sword. Your feet are shackled, and you are dragged away to the cheers of the crowd. It's not long before you find yourself chained to a wall of a dark dungeon cell, awaiting the arrival of the Earl of Kaad, who, you are told, will decide whether or not to hand you over to Lord Azzur. When he finally arrives, you can tell from the stern faces of Guards behind him that it is not good news. Your worst fears are confirmed when the Earl tells you solemnly that you will be taken in chains to Executioner's Square in Port Blacksand. Your adventure is over.

353

You break off another piece of honeycomb, but before you are able to eat the honey, you are engulfed by a swarm of angry bees. They begin stinging you all over, and painful red welts form on your skin. Lose 2 *STAMINA* points. If you want to try and fight them off, turn to **108**. If you would rather climb down the tree and run back to the beach to dive into the sea, turn to **336**.

354

When you come to, the market square is virtually deserted, and the old man is nowhere to be seen. You are annoyed at yourself for rashly attacking the Monk and you are even more annoyed when you discover that all your Gold Pieces have been taken. Lose 2 *LUCK* points. You pick yourself up and hobble across the market square to Clock Street. Turn to **140**.

355

You glance at the titles of the books on the shelves. They are all books on magic with intriguing titles like *The Secrets of Sorcerers* and *The Grimoire of Magic Missiles*, but the one that really catches your eye is a small, red leather-bound ancient tome held shut by a brass clasp. The book is entitled *The End of Time*, which is printed in large gold-leaf lettering on the cover. If you want to open the book, turn to **12**. If you want to walk up the stairs and go back outside, turn to **305**.

356

You feel a draught of cool air on your face caused by the door opening and quickly closing again. You hear a floorboard creak, which confirms somebody has entered the hut. If you want to call out to whoever it might be, turn to **281**. If you want to toss a coin on the floor to distract the intruder, turn to **100**.

357

Silence descends over the crowd. Azzur plays to the audience, rubbing his chin as though appearing to be deep in thought. "That's a good number," he says coldly. "But it's not good enough!" Turn to **25**.

358

You soon arrive at an old wooden hut, where you see a barrel on the porch with a note pinned to it which says POISON APPLE ALERT! HEALING POTIONS FOR SALE HERE. If you have recently eaten an apple and want to go in the hut, turn to **176**. If you want to carry on walking east, turn to **277**.

359

The Decayer spits at you as you run past it. *Test Your Luck*. If you are Lucky, turn to **17**. If you are Unlucky, turn to **131**.

360

The noise of your boots on the cobblestones is the only sound in the street. Everybody nearby turns to look at you, some of them pointing at your boots and putting their index fingers to their lips, gesturing for you to be quiet. Two high wooden gates up ahead on the right suddenly burst open, and a bare-chested GIANT storms out on to the street with a wooden club in his hand, his face contorted with rage. He is wearing a pair of ragged brown trousers tied at the waist with thick rope. Roaring with anger, he scans the street, looking for the person who disturbed his peace. He looks down, catches sight of your boots and raises his club in the air. You must battle the GIANT and ask questions later.

GIANT   *SKILL 8*   *STAMINA 9*

If you win, turn to **178**.

Your hopes of sailing away from danger are quickly dashed when a gigantic tentacle rises out of the sea, no more than twenty metres in front of you. Another tentacle rises out of the sea, then another, and another, until there are eight of them towering above you. Your boat is about to be attacked by a KRAKEN, a giant sea monster which has a colossal squid-like body, two huge eyes and a beaked mouth. You hear booming explosions from the pirate ship's cannon as two cannonballs whistle overhead towards the Kraken, one of them taking a big chunk out of one of its tentacles. The monster thrashes around in the sea and wraps one of its giant tentacles around the *Blue Moon*'s mast. It pulls the boat over and drags it down to the depths of the ocean with you on board. Your adventure is over.

A fearless and fanatical fighter armed with throwing spears

362

You ask the woman where she is going, and she replies that she's on her way to the general store to sell some arrows. She explains that she is a fletcher "by name and by profession". She claims to make the finest arrows in the land, saying, "Ask any bowman around here. They will all tell you that Frances Fletcher's arrows fly long and true. Would you like to buy some and save me the walk to the general store? They are only 2 Gold Pieces for six." If you want to buy six arrows, turn to **250**. If you would rather politely refuse her offer and carry on walking east, turn to **279**.

363

There is a gap up ahead in the tall grass on the right where a path joins the path you are on. A cloud of dust rises into the air from somebody or something running towards you along the path from the east. You reach the junction and see a tall, barefooted warrior woman sprinting towards you. She has striking silver markings covering much of her bronzed skin and her hair is close-cropped and dyed scarlet-red. She is a ZENGIAN ULTRA, a fearless and fanatical fighter armed with throwing spears. She lets out a shrill war cry and throws her spear at you. If you have a shield, turn to **2**. If you don't have a shield, turn to **169**.

364

After you pay him 5 Gold Pieces, the storekeeper hands you the food, which will add 4 *STAMINA* points when eaten. You put all your possessions into the Bag of Everything and marvel at how light it is. Combat will be easier from now on. Add 1 *SKILL* point. You thank the storekeeper and decide what to do next. If you want to ask him if he has heard of Garanka Vassell, turn to **229**. If you want to leave the store and head east on foot, turn to **203**.

365

There is a pile of stones in a dark recess in the cave wall. You remove the top layer and uncover a wooden chest with ornate brass hinges. You pick up the chest and carry it over to the mouth of the cave to examine it in the daylight. The lid is inlaid with a skull-and-crossbones motif made of mother-of-pearl. The chest does not appear to be locked. If you want to open the chest, turn to **56**. If you would rather scour the beach, turn to **231**.

366

"Nobody defies an order in the court of Sukumvit of Fang!" the Baron shouts out angrily. He snaps his fingers and his elite Guards rush forward to rain blow after blow down on you with their iron maces, clubbing you to the ground. Your hands are shackled behind your back, and you are made to stand bleeding and battered in front of the baying crowd to await your fate. Lord Azzur stares at you contemptuously, his head nodding slightly with satisfaction. The Baron turns to his guest and says, "My sincere apologies for this outrage, my dear Lord Azzur. As punishment, might I suggest we put this criminal in the iron gibbet hanging from the gallows in the town square and let the hungry crows do the rest?" Lord Azzur gives his approval with a simple gesture of the hand. You are dragged from the podium and you see Throm staring at you with a look of puzzlement on his face. What will become of him you will never know, but for you the gallows await. Your adventure is over.

367

You sit down on a bar stool and place your knife on the bar where everybody can see it. The innkeeper sidles up to you and says in a gruff, matter-of-fact voice, "Swords and knives are not allowed to be unsheathed in the Lobster. Hand it over." If you want to do as he says, turn to **84**. If you want to refuse to hand over your knife, turn to **253**.

368

You poke your head out from behind the tree and call out to the assassin. He replies by firing his crossbow, but the bolt thuds into the trunk of the tree. You hear him curse before disappearing from view. Moments later a heavily built man storms out of the tavern, screaming at the top of his voice, and charges at you like a raging bull, swinging a two-handed sword above his head. The deadly assassin is wearing a chain mail vest and you must fight him. Turn to **53**.

369

You hear a rustling sound in the long grass to your right. If you want to investigate, turn to **228**. If you would rather keep heading towards town, turn to **189**.

370

You climb carefully up the tree to where the hive is hanging from a branch. You hear a faint buzzing sound, but you are fairly certain there can only be a few bees inside the hive. You poke the tip of your sword inside and break off a piece of honeycomb. You reach into the hive and pull out the honeycomb, which is dripping with thick golden honey. Slavering in anticipation, you cram a chunk of the honeycomb into your mouth, sucking out the deliciously sweet nectar and feeling instantly energized. Add 2 *STAMINA* points. You are about to break off another piece of honeycomb when you hear the ominous buzzing sound of the swarm of bees returning to the hive. If you want to reach for the honeycomb, turn to **353**. If you would rather climb quickly down the tree and run back to your hut, turn to **147**.

371

The blacksmith's bushy eyebrows rise up when you tell him about your recent encounters with Lord Azzur's assassins. "That is terrible!" he says with genuine concern. "Azzur was in Kaad yesterday, spreading lies and buying favours. A plague be on him. I put new shoes on his carriage horse and he didn't bother paying me before leaving town. I'm not sure if it has anything to do with you, but he had two people with him who he dropped off. One was a woman in a red hooded cloak. Her icy stare made me feel quite uncomfortable. Ruth was her name. Red Ruth. The other was a short, stocky man with narrow eyes who looked like he was from the East, maybe Kay-Pong. I remember he was carrying a black stick and had a strange name. I think Azzur called him Tunku Yang." You thank the blacksmith for the information and go back outside to walk down the side passage. Turn to **330**.

372

You stand up and tell Sidd that you are not going to pay him. "That's not very nice of you," he says with a hurt expression on his face. "You might live to regret that decision. Or you might not live long enough to regret it!" Sidd turns his back on you and stares out of the window. A black cat suddenly jumps on to the bar and stares at you and hisses. Lose 1 *LUCK* point. Tall Tom has a face like thunder, and points at the door and tells you to leave. You walk outside and think about which way to go. If you want to head north, turn to **133**. If you want to continue east, turn to **157**.

373

The lightning strikes the sea a short distance away, but it is too close for comfort for Captain Crow. "I'm turning the boat around whether you like it or not," he screams at you into the wind. "We're going back to Snake Island!" He pulls on the tiller with all his might, forcing the mainsail to swing across the deck as the boat goes about, shuddering noisily when the ropes twang taut in their cleats. Battling against the giant waves, the captain looks relieved to be heading back, but it is another hour before you make landfall, just as the wind dies down. The captain looks at you and says sternly, "I don't care what you say, we're staying on the island tonight!" You nod in agreement and praise the captain for getting you back to the island safely, and suggest you make a fire to get warm. Turn to **302**.

374

The man stumbles when firing his crossbow and a small arrow thumps into the wall behind you. Realizing there is no time for him to reload his crossbow, he draws a sabre from his belt and lunges at you, shouting, "I, Blackthorn of Chalice, will see your head delivered to Lord Azzur." You must fight him.

BLACKTHORN   *SKILL 8*   *STAMINA 7*

If you win, turn to **109**.

375

The boat man pulls out a small leather purse from his clothing and counts out 20 Gold Pieces into your hand. "That's a fair price for a fair boat," he says, smiling. He shakes your hand, bids you farewell, and walks back into his yard, whistling happily with his dogs following faithfully behind. If you now want to go in the general store, turn to **327**. If you would rather head east on foot, turn to **203**.

376

Your backpack is weighing you down and the Orcs are closing in fast. If you want to drop your backpack, turn to **83**. If you want to keep on running with it on, turn to **8**.

377

You shake the silver box and hear something rattle inside. You open it up and find two small sparkling diamonds. Add 1 *LUCK* point. You close the lid and put the box in your pocket. There are also two small corked bottles in the chest. One is a clear glass bottle containing red ink. The other is a brown bottle with a label on it with the words "Worm Paste" handwritten in faded red ink. You must decide whether or not to keep the bottles. If you have not done so already, you can either open the leather purse (turn to **319**) or scour the beach in the hope of finding something useful (turn to **231**).

378

Your walk along the trail is uneventful and you reach the banks of the River Kok by late morning. The river is wide and fast-running. Looking north, you see the town of Fang set against the stunning backdrop of the snow-capped Icefinger Mountains in the distance. Just to your right, there is a small wooden hut close to a wooden jetty which has a rowing boat tied to it. There is somebody lying in the boat who appears to be asleep. If you want to ring the brass bell on the pier to wake the sleeping man, turn to **39**. If you want to look inside the hut, turn to **297**.

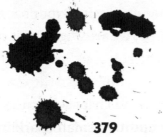

379

The pain gradually increases, building in intensity until it is unbearable. Your heart pounds inside your chest, beating faster and faster until you think it is about to explode. You scream in agony before blacking out, and never regain consciousness. Your adventure is over.

380

The man looks at you intensely, as though trying to remember where he's seen you before. He frowns and purses his lips in thought, and says, "I might be interested, it depends. You better show me the boat." You lead the man to the *Blue Moon*. He jumps on board and inspects it briefly for seaworthiness. "She's a fine boat, no doubt about it, but the last time I saw the *Blue Moon*, she belonged to Samuel Crow. I can't imagine old Sam would ever sell her. How come you claim to be the owner?" If you want to reply that Captain Crow died on Snake Island, turn to **136**. If you want to reply that you won the boat from the captain playing cards, turn to **338**.

381

Billy stares down at you and says, "We don't like what we are hearing, stranger. If you can't do right by us, we can't do right by you. So, we are going to let you play Beat-the-Buss. These are the rules, so listen carefully. Brother Bobby and I are going to climb on to the roof. I should tell you he's got a blunderbuss. That's where the buss in Beat-the-Buss comes from, as in blunderbuss, if you're getting me? I'm going to throw you a rope and count to twenty before brother Bobby starts shooting. All you have to do is climb out and hightail it for the wooden gate without being shot full of lead. Are you understanding me? Don't try any funny business or brother Bobby will shoot you right here and now." The brothers disappear and seconds later a thick length of rope drops down into the cellar. You catch hold of it and give it a tug. Satisfied it will bear your weight, you haul yourself out of the cellar. There is a ladder leading up to a skylight in the roof, through which you hear a voice counting, "Twelve ... thirteen ... fourteen..." and realize you must run for your life. You bolt for the door and run out of the farmhouse and down the path as fast as you can. If you are wearing Elven Boots, turn to **90**. If you are not wearing Elven Boots, turn to **323**.

382

Half an hour later, you finally get a tug on your fishing line. *Test Your Luck.* If you are Lucky, turn to **278**. If you are Unlucky, turn to **142**.

383

The man puts his hands together and says, "It's about time! I thought you were never going to arrive. Please come in. My cellar is infested with rats. I think they are getting in through a broken drain. The cellar is at the bottom of the stairs, which are through the door at the back of the room over there." You walk over to the door and go down a stone staircase to another door at the bottom. You listen at the door and hear lots of scratching and squeaking sounds coming from the other side. You open the door to a storeroom where you see hundreds of rats crawling all over the shelves, sacks, boxes and barrels in the room. If you have a flute, turn to **280**. If you do not have a flute, turn to **219**.

384

You hand over your boots to the Gnome, who hurriedly kicks off his old boots and pulls the new ones on. He stands up and runs around in a circle, clapping his hands with glee. He gives you 1 Gold Piece and asks you where you are going. You reply that you are heading north on a mission. "Well, if you haven't been there before, you should definitely visit Kaad since you are heading that way. You won't forget it. The people who live there are pig-poo crazy!" You thank the Gnome for his advice and set off again. Turn to **179**.

385

You climb over the side of the boat and lie down in the bottom. *Test Your Luck*. If you are Lucky, turn to **209**. If you are Unlucky, turn to **134**.

386

Balthazar's eyes light up at the mention of the box. He clasps his hands together and says, "What wonderful news! The box was stolen from here yesterday and I thought I was never going to see it again. Please come in." You follow Balthazar into a large stone-walled room which has a door in the far wall. You take the wooden box out of your backpack and place it on the table in the centre of the room. "I'm going to open the box, so please stand back. There is a secret spring-loaded dart in the catch which I'm going to disable. There, it's done," Balthazar says with a relieved expression on his face. He empties the contents of the box on to the table, which amount to 10 Gold Pieces, two long brass clock hands and a gold signet ring with a question mark engraved on it. "The new clock hands are safe! What a relief. I cannot thank you enough. Please accept 5 Gold Pieces as a reward," he says cheerfully. You accept the Gold Pieces and watch Balthazar start to polish the clock hands feverishly. If you want to ask if he has seen Lord Azzur in town, turn to **167**. If you would rather bid him farewell and turn right up Clock Street, turn to **89**.

387

You are exhausted after the long sword fight and take a moment to get your breath back. You empty Vassell's pockets and find 3 Gold Pieces. When you pull down his tunic collar, you see the now familiar scorpion assassin pendant hanging on a chain around his neck. You snap the chain and put the pendant in your pocket. Will you now:

Try on his chain mail vest?	Turn to **246**
Go in the tavern?	Turn to **341**
Head north along a new path?	Turn to **133**
Continue your journey east?	Turn to **157**

The beggar continues to rattle his tin mug

388

You land on a patch of soft sand and injure yourself, suffering a twisted ankle and a cracked rib. Lose 2 *SKILL* points and 4 *STAMINA* points. If you are still alive, turn to **392**.

389

With his head bowed, the beggar continues to rattle his tin mug. As soon as you put your hand in your pocket to find a coin, he drops his mug and throws off his blanket to reveal a sword held in the hand you thought was missing! With steely-cold eyes and a sinister smile, he lunges forward with his sword and stabs you in the leg. Lose 2 *STAMINA* points. Your attacker is an ELITE SWORDSMAN who lunges forward to strike you again.

ELITE SWORDSMAN   *SKILL 8*   *STAMINA 5*

If you win, turn to **190**.

390

As the carriage passes by, the woman looks down at you from her bench seat and says in a cold voice, "I know who you are." But before you can say anything, the driver cracks his whip and urges his horse into a trot and the carriage disappears in a cloud of dust. Wondering who the woman might be, you walk through the main gates and mingle with the townsfolk, who are busily going about their various tasks. Nobody pays you much attention and you walk down Crown Street, which is lined on both sides with small shops and old wood and plaster houses with tiled roofs. The street leads you to a market square, where the traders are packing up their stalls for the day. You see a portly man in long brown robes walking towards you carrying a large sack over his shoulder. If you want to talk to him, turn to **19**. If you would rather ignore him and walk across the market square to Clock Street, turn to **140**.

391

As you run for the cover of the trees and undergrowth, the giant Dragon swoops down to blast you with its fiery breath. *Test Your Luck*. If you are Lucky, turn to **236**. If you are Unlucky, turn to **172**.

392

You look up to see the Flesh-Head peering down over

the cliff edge, snarling aggressively. You stand up in considerable pain, and limp slowly over to the mouth of the cave. Turn to **201**.

393

You don't speak to the pirate during the voyage, and it's only when the old buildings of Port Blacksand finally come into view that you tell him that you are going to set him free, even though he does not deserve it. You untie him and tell him to swim to the shore. He protests, but you boot him overboard and sail on. It's not long before you are moored up alongside the harbour wall of the old port, notorious for the pirates, cutthroats and thieves who live there. Two rough-looking men with missing teeth and stubbly beards are standing on the quayside, watching you closely, and start whispering to each other. It's only a few days since you were last here, but now you can't afford to trust anybody. If you want to ask them if they know somebody who might want to buy your boat, turn to **48**. If you want to walk quickly past them and enter the Black Lobster Tavern at the end of the quay, turn to **334**.

394

You shout out the magic spell just in time as the band of bloodthirsty Orcs descends upon you, screaming loudly as though possessed by demons. You disappear from view and manage to escape from the Orcs, who are now even more angry and start fighting between themselves. You run northwards to get as far away as possible from the Orcs before the invisibility spell wears off. A minute later your limbs and torso become visible again. You look back and are relieved to see that the Orc hunting party is still embroiled in a mass brawl. Just when you think you're clear of them, a long blast on a hunting horn signals that you have been spotted by one of their scouts. The Orcs stop fighting and chase after you, screaming for your blood. All you can do is run! If you are wearing Elven Boots, turn to **241**. If you are wearing ordinary leather boots, turn to **18**.

395

You have picked up a cursed stone carving known as the Evil Eye. Lose 3 *LUCK* points. Unaware that you have found an unlucky artefact, you place it in your backpack and carry on your search for food. Turn to **213**.

396

As you approach the crossroads with Bell Street and Clock Street, you notice that some of the people are armed with clubs and pitchforks. You suspect they are probably looking for you. Pretending to scratch your hair, you raise an arm to hide your face and turn right into Clock Street, hoping not to be recognized. *Test Your Luck*. If you are Lucky, turn to **207**. If you are Unlucky, turn to **284**.

397

Try as you might, you are unable to open the jaws of the animal trap. Your ankle goes numb, and you feel a throbbing pain in your lower leg. Lose 2 *STAMINA* points. As the day wears on you begin to wonder how long you will have to wait before the trapper returns to examine his trap. You decide to start calling out in the hope of attracting help. *Test Your Luck*. If you are Lucky, turn to **128**. If you are Unlucky, turn to **205**.

398

You have no idea how long you have been in a semi-coma, but you eventually cool down and wake up. You feel incredibly weak, and have trouble standing up. You stretch out your arms and see that your hands are trembling. Lose 1 *SKILL* point. You are about to set off again when you notice an iron bracelet lying in the earth near the entrance of the den. If you want to try on the bracelet, turn to **40**. If you would rather leave it where it is and head back to your hut on the other side of the island, turn to **217**.

399

You watch the arrow fly towards the open window, but it strikes the frame, missing its target. Lose 1 *LUCK* point. Before you have time to fire another arrow, the tavern door bursts open. A heavily built man wearing a chain mail vest storms out of the tavern, screaming at the top of his voice, and charges at you like a raging bull swinging a two-handed sword above his head. You draw your sword and ready yourself to fight the deadly assassin, Garanka Vassell. Turn to **53**.

400

Baron Sukumvit raises his arm aloft for the trumpets to sound the start of this year's Trial of Champions. The crowd cheers loudly, and one by one the contestants salute the Baron and disappear inside the dungeon. You see Throm enter third, and when your turn comes, you are greeted by a wall of noise from the excited crowd. You salute them briefly and draw your sword before stepping through the ornate stone-pillared entrance to the dark dungeon. You curse Lord Azzur's name under your breath and promise yourself that one day you will see him dead. For now, the toughest challenge of your life awaits you as you step into the unknown to face Baron Sukumvit's deadly traps and gruesome monsters.

HOW TO FIGHT
THE CREATURES OF
ASSASSINS OF ALLANSIA

YOU have been preparing for your quest by practising your swordplay and building up your strength and stamina. You have a sword and a backpack containing Provisions (food and drink) to sustain you through your adventure. Before setting of on your adventure, you must first roll dice to record your *SKILL, STAMINA* and *LUCK* scores on your *Adventure Sheet* on pages 248 or 250, which you should also use to keep a record of the items you find on your adventure. Use the *Monster Encounter Sheet* to record combat with monsters. Write your scores in pencil or make photocopies of the blank *Adventure Sheet* to use in future adventures.

SKILL, STAMINA AND LUCK

To determine your *Initial SKILL*, *STAMINA* and *LUCK* scores:

Roll one die. Add 6 to this number and enter this total in the *SKILL* box on the *Adventure Sheet*.

Roll both dice. Add 12 to the number rolled and enter this total in the *STAMINA* box.

Roll one die, add 6 to this number and enter this total in the *LUCK* box.

SKILL reflects your swordsmanship and fighting expertise; the higher the better. *STAMINA* represents your strength; the higher your *STAMINA*, the longer you will survive. *LUCK* represents how lucky a person you are. Luck – and magic – are facts of life in the fantasy world you are about to explore.

SKILL, *STAMINA* and *LUCK* scores change constantly during an adventure, so keep an eraser handy. You must keep an accurate record of these scores. But never rub out your *initial scores*. Although you may receive additional *SKILL*, *STAMINA* and *LUCK* points, these totals may never exceed your *initial* scores, except on very rare occasions, when instructed on a particular page.

BATTLES

When you are told to fight a creature, you must resolve the battle as described below. First record the creature's *SKILL* and *STAMINA* SCORES (as given on the page) in an empty *Monster Encounter Box* on your *Adventure Sheet*. The sequence of combat is then:

1. Roll the two dice for the creature. Add its *SKILL* score.

This total is the **creature's** *Attack Strength*.

2. Roll the two dice for yourself. Add your current *SKILL*. This total is **your** *Attack Strength*.

3. Whose *Attack Strength* is higher? If your *Attack Strength* is higher, you have wounded the creature. If the creature's *Attack Strength* is higher, it has wounded you. (If both are the same, you have both missed – start the next *Attack Round* from step 1 above.)

4. If you wounded the creature, subtract 2 points from the **creature's** *STAMINA* score. You may use *LUCK* here to do additional damage (see "Using Luck in Battles" below).

5. If the creature wounded you, subtract 2 points from **your** *STAMINA* score. You may use *LUCK* to minimize the damage (see below).

6. Make the appropriate changes to either the creature's or your own *STAMINA* scores (and your *LUCK* score if you used LUCK) and begin the next *Attack Round* (repeat steps 1–6)

7. This continues until the *STAMINA* score of either you or creature you are fighting has been reduced to zero (death).

LUCK

Sometimes you will be told to *Test Your Luck*. As you will discover, using *LUCK* is a risky business. The way you *Test Your Luck* is as follows:

Roll two dice. If the number rolled is equal to or less than your current *LUCK* score, you have been *Lucky*. If the number rolled is higher than your current *LUCK* score, you have been *Unlucky*. The consequences of being *Lucky* or *Unlucky* will be found in the paragraph you are sent to. Each time you *Test Your Luck,* you must subtract one point from your current *LUCK* score. So, the more you rely on luck, the riskier this becomes.

Using Luck in Battles

In battles, you always have the option of using your LUCK either to score a more serious wound on a creature, or to minimize the effects of a wound on the creature has just scored on you.

If you have just wounded the creature: you may *Test Your Luck* as described below. If you are *Lucky,* subtract an extra 2 points from the creature's *STAMINA* score (i.e., 4 instead of 2 normally). But if you are *Unlucky,* you must restore 1 point to the creature's *STAMINA* (so instead of scoring the normal 2 points of damage, you have now only scored 1).

If you have just been wounded by the creature: you may *Test Your Luck* to try to minimize the wound. If you are *Lucky*, restore 1 point of your *STAMINA* (i.e., instead of doing 2 points of damage, it has done only 1). If you are *Unlucky*, subtract 1 extra *STAMINA* point.

Don't forget to subtract 1 point from your *LUCK* score each time you *Test Your Luck*.

RESTORING SKILL, STAMINA AND LUCK

Skill

Occasionally, a page may give instructions to alter your *SKILL* score. A Magic Weapon may increase your *SKILL*, but remember that only one weapon can be used at a time! You cannot claim 2 *SKILL* bonuses for carrying two Magic Swords. Your *SKILL* score can never exceed its *initial* value unless specifically instructed. Drinking the Potion of Skill (see later) will restore your *SKILL* to its initial level at any time.

Stamina and Provisions

Your *STAMINA* score will change a lot during the adventure. As you near your goal, your *STAMINA* level may become dangerously low and battles may be particularly risky, so be careful!

You start the game with enough Provisions for ten meals

(see "Equipment and Potions" below). A separate *Provisions Remaining* box is provided on the *Adventure Sheet* for recording details of Provisions. You may eat only *one* meal at a time. When you eat a meal, add 4 points to your *STAMINA* score and deduct 1 point from your Provisions. Remember that you have a long way to go, so use your Provisions wisely!

Don't forget that your *STAMINA* score may never exceed its *initial* value unless specifically instructed on a page. Drinking the Potion of Strength (see later) will restore your *STAMINA* to its *initial* level at any time.

Luck

You will find additions to your *LUCK* score awarded when you have been particularly *Lucky*. Remember that, as with *SKILL* and *STAMINA*, your *LUCK* score may never exceed its *initial* value unless specifically instructed on a page. Drinking the Potion of Fortune (see later) will restore your *LUCK* to its *initial* level at any time and increase your *initial LUCK* by 1 point.

EQUIPMENT AND POTIONS

You begin your adventure with a sword and a backpack containing Provisions (food and drink). You will find gold, treasure, weapons, armour and artefacts on your adventure. But not all items will help you on your quest. Some might even harm you!

You may also take a magic potion which will aid you on your quest. Each bottle of potion contains enough for *one* measure, i.e., it can only be used *once* during an adventure. Choose ONE of the following:

A Potion of Skill – restores *SKILL* points

A Potion of Strength – restores *STAMINA* points

A Potion of Fortune – restores *LUCK* points and adds 1 to *Initial LUCK*

These potions may be taken at any time during the adventure. Taking a measure of potion will restore *SKILL*, *STAMINA* or *LUCK* scores to their *Initial* level. The Potion of Fortune will increase your *Initial LUCK* score by 1 point and restore *LUCK* to this new *Initial* level.

HINTS ON PLAY

There is only one true way through **Assassins of Allansia** and it will probably take you several attempts to find it. Make notes and draw a map as you explore – this map will be useful in future adventures and help you identify unexplored areas.

Not all locations contain treasure; many merely contain traps and creatures. There are many "wild-goose chase" passages, and while you may progress through to your ultimate destination, it is by no means certain that you will win.

The "one true way" involves a minimum of risk and any player, no matter how weak their initial dice rolls might be, should be able to get through.

Good LUCK on your adventure – you'll need it!

ADVENTURE SHEET

| SKILL ☐ | STAMINA ☐ | LUCK ☐ |

BACKPACK ITEMS:	POCKET ITEMS:	GOLD PIECES:
	PENDANTS:	WEAPONS:
	PROVISIONS:	ARMOUR:

ENEMY ENCOUNTER SHEET

| SKILL ☐ | SKILL ☐ | SKILL ☐ | SKILL ☐ |
| STAMINA ☐ | STAMINA ☐ | STAMINA ☐ | STAMINA ☐ |

| SKILL ☐ | SKILL ☐ | SKILL ☐ | SKILL ☐ |
| STAMINA ☐ | STAMINA ☐ | STAMINA ☐ | STAMINA ☐ |

| SKILL ☐ | SKILL ☐ | SKILL ☐ | SKILL ☐ |
| STAMINA ☐ | STAMINA ☐ | STAMINA ☐ | STAMINA ☐ |

| SKILL ☐ | SKILL ☐ | SKILL ☐ | SKILL ☐ |
| STAMINA ☐ | STAMINA ☐ | STAMINA ☐ | STAMINA ☐ |

| SKILL ☐ | SKILL ☐ | SKILL ☐ | SKILL ☐ |
| STAMINA ☐ | STAMINA ☐ | STAMINA ☐ | STAMINA ☐ |

| SKILL ☐ | SKILL ☐ | SKILL ☐ | SKILL ☐ |
| STAMINA ☐ | STAMINA ☐ | STAMINA ☐ | STAMINA ☐ |

ADVENTURE SHEET

SKILL		STAMINA		LUCK	

BACKPACK ITEMS:

POCKET ITEMS:

GOLD PIECES:

PENDANTS:

WEAPONS:

PROVISIONS:

ARMOUR:

ENEMY ENCOUNTER SHEET

SKILL ☐	SKILL ☐	SKILL ☐	SKILL ☐
STAMINA ☐	STAMINA ☐	STAMINA ☐	STAMINA ☐

SKILL ☐	SKILL ☐	SKILL ☐	SKILL ☐
STAMINA ☐	STAMINA ☐	STAMINA ☐	STAMINA ☐

SKILL ☐	SKILL ☐	SKILL ☐	SKILL ☐
STAMINA ☐	STAMINA ☐	STAMINA ☐	STAMINA ☐

SKILL ☐	SKILL ☐	SKILL ☐	SKILL ☐
STAMINA ☐	STAMINA ☐	STAMINA ☐	STAMINA ☐

SKILL ☐	SKILL ☐	SKILL ☐	SKILL ☐
STAMINA ☐	STAMINA ☐	STAMINA ☐	STAMINA ☐

SKILL ☐	SKILL ☐	SKILL ☐	SKILL ☐
STAMINA ☐	STAMINA ☐	STAMINA ☐	STAMINA ☐

YOU ARE THE HERO

F F
FIGHTING FANTASY

DEATHTRAP DUNGEON

IAN LIVINGSTONE

Devised by the devilish mind of Baron Sukumvit, the labyrinth of Fang plays host to the Trial of Champions – a challenge that no adventurer ever survived. You'll have to pit your wits against some fiendish foes if you have any hope of seeing daylight again...

YOU ARE THE HERO

FIGHTING FANTASY

THE
FOREST
OF
DOOM

IAN LIVINGSTONE

A war is raging and your help is needed to vanquish the evil trolls. To save the dwarfs, you must find the grand wizard Yaztromo and track down the pieces of a legendary war hammer lost in the depths of Darkwood Forest, where gruesome monsters lurk...

You, the hero, are tasked with confronting the terrifying Lizard King and freeing the human slaves captured by his bloodthirsty army. You must discover the chink in his armour if you have any hope of defeating him...

YOU ARE THE HERO

FIGHTING FANTASY

COLLECT THEM ALL, BRAVE ADVENTURER!

WARLOCK of FIRETOP MOUNTAIN
STEVE JACKSON
IAN LIVINGSTONE

CITY of THIEVES
IAN LIVINGSTONE

CITADEL of CHAOS
STEVE JACKSON

FOREST of DOOM
IAN LIVINGSTONE

HOUSE of HELL
STEVE JACKSON

PORT PERIL
IAN LIVINGSTONE

DEATHTRAP DUNGEON
IAN LIVINGSTONE

CREATURE of HAVOC
STEVE JACKSON

ISLAND of the LIZARD KING
IAN LIVINGSTONE

STEVE JACKSON

SORCERY! SHAMUTANTI HILLS
STEVE JACKSON

GATES of DEATH
CHARLIE HIGSON

CAVERNS of the SNOW WITCH
IAN LIVINGSTONE

SORCERY! CITYPORT of TRAPS
STEVE JACKSON

ASSASSINS of ALLANSIA
IAN LIVINGSTONE